KREW ENTERTAINMENT GROUP
PRESENTS

CRACK'IN

KEVIN WHITAKER

McClure Publishing, Inc.

CRACK' IN by Kevin Whitaker - Copyright © 2017

~ ~ ~

The author and publisher have made every effort to ensure the accuracy and completeness of information contained in this book. We assume no responsibility for errors, inaccuracies, omissions, or any inconsistencies therein.

ISBN 13: 978-0-9989223-3-1

Cover Design Images by: David Dickerson.

Interior Layout by Kathy McClure

https://www.mcclurepublishing.com

To order additional copies, please contact

books@mcclurepublishing.com
800-659-4908

ACKNOWLEDGEMENTS

Krew Entertainment Group, McClure Publishing, Inc., L. Johns Law Group, Live Club Link, Western Auto Repair, Men@Large, LeClaire Community, Kell's Dougie, Parker Trucking, The Tate Brothers, M.O.B., Corner Crew, Will Do Krew, 45th Lawler Click, Marlene's Beauty Salon, Buns Unlimited Inc. Pough Transportation, Mad Capital LLC, Parsat Electronics, Diva Dolls International, Design Studios Inc., Eminence Professional Development, Bernina Bijou (Editor), and Sista Girlz (Book Club).

SPECIAL THANKS

To God for blessing me with a loving family and friends, Dr. A. Johnson and family, my sisters Karla, Yvette, Ashley, and brothers Victor and Gerald. My daughters Tara, Felicia, Kiandra, Natasha, Kyleishia, Cindy, my name sake Kevin Whitaker Jr., My Auntie Edna Fuller and family, The Whitakers family, Uncle Ted, Uncle Ralph, Uncle James, Auntie Velma, Auntie Wakanda, Auntie Evonne, The Whitaker in (St. Louis, Kansas City and Chicago,) Bernina McKennie (Editor), Leyte Holliday (artist) and family, Simona (Bambina) Jackson (model) and family, Dave Tolliver (R&B singer) and Edgar (Gemini) Porter, Mrs. M. Boulware and family, Ramona Hopkins and family, Mrs. V. West and family, Mrs. Esther Singleton and family, Mr. and Mrs. Noble, Herb Coleman, Roslyn Carson and family, Eddo, ES Blue, Dreek, Quik-Mix-Claude, DJ Jermaine (The Gentleman), DJ. Eight-Ball, DJ Art, Jay Honey, and a host of others. To all my people who have supported my craft MUCH LOVE TO YOU AND MAY GOD CONTINUE TO BLESS YOU.

FOREWORD

Billions of dollars are being wired all over the world within minutes. Your life savings could be gone in a matter of seconds.

Welcome to the fast life where everything you love could be gone in the blink of an eye. Imagine a world that is controlled by technology. From smartphones to computers, everything can be saved and erased but never forgotten. Octavius Smith is a highly skilled computer store worker with high credentials, working under a boss who knows very little about the company he runs. Octavius discovers the truth about one of their more frequent customers. He isn't who he says he is.

Several times a month, Octavius sits behind the counter and watches customers walk in and out of the shop feeling a little better about their understanding of technology. In the crowd, there is always one person who catches his attention ... Chris Miller. Or maybe it was Mr. James Brown? Perhaps even Mr. Tate?

Crack'in will have you thinking about, "Who's in your wallet?" Don't' even waste time trying to answer the question. By the time you process what you just read, it's already on and *Crack'in*!

INTRODUCTION

Crack'in takes place in two major cities, Chicago and Uptown New York. On this beautiful sunny morning traffic is heavy. Octavius Smith works in a computer store as the number one computer repairman. He's running late for work, and traffic is barely moving. He tries to exit off the expressway when he is suddenly cut off by a late model blue Corvette. He quickly maneuvers to the right just stopping his minivan from hitting the guardrail. He spills hot Starbucks coffee on his leg. "AHHH!" He angrily gains control of his vehicle trying to catch up with the late model Corvette. He glances at the time. Already late for work, he pursues the Corvette. A traffic light has caught the Corvette, and Octavius is just two cars back. At this time, all Octavius could see was a young lady in the passenger seat looking back at him giving him the middle finger laughing. Octavius quickly retrieves his laptop from his bag powering it up in seconds. Traffic starts to move, and the Corvette begins to pull away. Octavius, furious, that he got caught by the red light. As the Corvette continues on, he ponders the thought of running the light, but thought better of it after looking up at the red light camera. He is upset and continues on to work just as he turns the corner two blocks away from the job. He sees the blue Corvette while sitting at the light. The Corvette is parked. As he drives pass, he jots down the license plate number. Octavius dials up North Star.

"Thank you for calling North Star. How may I assist you today?" the North Star operator asked.

Octavius, frantically, says, "I just witnessed a carjacking, license plate UE 507, late model blue Corvette. A guy and a girl just jumped inside of this parked car pushing the man to the ground."

"Give me one second, Sir." Octavius, cracking up laughing on the inside, circles the block a couple times. "Sir, that vehicle has just been shut down and the police are in route. Please hold, Sir, so that I may get your name and number."

He circles the block one final time, and the police have the car surrounded. He pulls up really slow so the passenger and driver can see his face. He has a big grin and his middle finger up. He shuts his laptop computer and drives away.

Octavius finally arrives to work 45 minutes late. His boss, Mr. Stanley Fisher, is very irate when Octavius steps in the door.

"Where the hell have you been?" Stanley Fisher asked.

"The traffic was terrible today," Octavius replies, as he strolls passed his boss to put away his things.

"Work starts at eight o'clock sharp? Be here or be looking for another job!" Mr. Fisher said angrily.

Octavius slides his backpack off his shoulders, as the customers just listen and observe. Mr. Fisher gets a full view of Octavius instantly going nuts.

"WHAT THE HELL IS THAT BIG STAIN ON YOUR PANTS? Not only are you late, but your uniform is dirty! Mr. Fisher says, angrily. "Oh My Lord! What is the world coming too?" Mr. Fisher walks away mumbling under his breath.

Octavius puts on his smock thinking to himself, *If your father didn't own a chain of computer repair shops, you couldn't get a job. You're about as smart as a box of rocks.* He giggles to himself stepping up to the counter. The door chimes and a young lady comes in the store looking around. She walks up to the counter and introduces herself, "Hi! My name is Cassie."

Octavius admiring Cassie's beauty, "So how may I help you?"

Cassie wearing a long summer coat steps away from the counter revealing a swimsuit that catches everyone in the store off guard. "I want to start my own swimsuit calendar and website. What would it take? Can you help me?" Cassie asked.

Mr. Fisher quickly interrupts, "Yes, he can help you. He's a Web Designer. Just call him 'Web Head'." Mr. Fisher giggles.

Cassie doesn't get the joke and with a confused look, "I don't follow?"

Another customer steps to the counter ready to check out. He's very well dressed, wearing a very expensive Hugo Boss suit, Rolex watch, and extremely well groomed. He appears to be in his late 20s, carrying three computer monitors while talking on his cell phone through his Bluetooth. There are a couple of large flat screen televisions set up around the store and one behind the counter showing the news.

Octavius pleasantly smiles, "Will that be all for you today, Sir?"

He raises his finger indicating for Octavius to give him a second while he continues his phone call. He giggles. "Okay, Jerry, I'll do just that!" He ends the call by touching his Bluetooth. Mr. Fisher notices the large purchase about to be made by the gentleman and takes the sale away from Octavius.

"Sir, you can step right down, if you're ready to check out," Mr. Fisher says. The gentleman ignores Mr. Fisher looking at the television monitor. At that moment "Breaking News" appears on the screen. Mr. Fisher quickly grabs the remote turning up the volume.

"Hi! I'm Jim Randle reporting live from Ohio and State Street on this beautiful morning. As you can see there are squad cars everywhere in this alleged carjacking. An anonymous call was made to North Star indicating that there had been a carjacking of some sort. When the police arrived on location, they found a high school coach with an underage cheerleader. The car was found to belong to the coach, but now there's an investigation underway about the underage cheerleader being in the car."

"So you telling me that we went from a carjacking to an underage cheerleader? Both are some very serious charges," Karen, the anchorwoman, says from the station.

"You're right, Karen; however, the police are more concerned now about where the call came from. I'm Jim Randle reporting live from downtown Chicago."

Octavius burst out loudly laughing. Cassie unamused with a perplexed look, "What's so funny?"

Octavius laughs it off. "You would have had to been there."

Mr. Stanley Fisher has the gentleman at the register ringing up his items. "Sir, your total comes to $540. Will that be cash or credit? Before you decide, can I interest you in an extended warranty?"

"No, thanks, and that will be credit."

"Okay, I'm going to need to see an ID please." The gentleman reaches in his pocket passing his identification to Mr. Fisher. "Okay, Mr. Brown. Go ahead and swipe your card." Mr. Brown swipes his card.

"So that's James Brown like the singer?" Mr. Fisher asked. He hands the receipt over to Mr. Brown to sign.

"No, it's James Brown like my father's name," Mr. Brown replied.

Stanley Fisher, kind of excited, "James Brown was your father?"

Mr. Brown picks up his bags, "No! James Brown is my father and not deceased. What a Dork! I'm a 30-year-old white guy with a Miami tan." He walks over and gives Octavius and Cassie one of his business cards, continues out the door shaking his head. Octavius has a silly grin on his face when Mr. Fisher turns around.

Mr. Fisher embarrassed, "What are you looking at? Hell ... James Brown dated white women. Help the next customer, Geek!"

Later on that week Mr. Brown is sitting in his downtown condo looking out over Lake Michigan. He's sitting in the office looking over credit cards while talking on his speakerphone. He chuckles, "Ha Ha ... I know that you're going to make that happen for me, right?"

The caller says, "There's no doubt about it. Have I ever let you down?"

Mr. Brown holds the credit card in the air to observe the front and back. "No, you haven't let me down. Let's just keep it that way."

"That's what I do. Keep it right. I'll get back to you when it's done."

Brown is about to disconnect the call glancing at a stack of credit cards on his desk. At that very moment the other line signals. He looks on the phone not recognizing the number he pauses before answering. He answers very professionally, "Hello! How may I help you?"

Octavius very excited, "Hey Dude! It's me from the computer store, Octavius."

"How's it going?" Brown asked.

"It's good. Just seeing what's happening in your day," Octavius replied.

Brown gives a slight chuckle, "Let me clear this other call."

Brown switches back over, "Hey, Eric. We still on for lunch this week? Go ahead book a five-star restaurant then text me the information. I'll take care of the bill from this end. Cool?"

Eric agrees, "Okay, my brother. I'm on that."

Brown clicks back over to the other line to the sound of people cheering. "Dude, you there?" Brown asked.

Octavius out of breath, "Yeah, Dude! WOO!!"

"What's all that noise in the background?"

"Dude, I'm down here at the skateboard park."

"Skateboard park? Dude, are you serious?" Brown asked.

At the skateboard park it's a warm sunny day. The park is packed as Octavius is sitting on the bench watching skateboarders do their stunts.

"Yes, Sir, I'm not as good as I used to be, but I still got it."

"How about we go out for a bite this evening? I've got something that I want to run by you." Brown asked.

Octavius's relaxing on the bench trying to catch his breath. "Okay, let's do it. Where?"

"The steak house right off Canal. About 7:30," Brown stated.

Octavius glances at the time, "Cutting it close, but I should be showered and cleaned up by then."

The phone call ended. Octavius looks at his phone. "Rude Dude!" He hops up jumping on his skateboard headed home. He's about to pass some of the younger skateboarders when he tries to do a trick falling busting his butt. He lies on the ground embarrassed as the other skaters laugh hysterically, "Goof Troop!" He had to laugh at himself as he thought back telling Brown he still had it.

Later that evening Brown is sitting at the table waiting on Octavius' arrival. He strolls through his phone when the waiter approaches. "Excuse me, Sir. I think your guest has arrived. However, he is not dressed appropriately for this establishment."

Brown nods his head in disapproval, "Is there anything I can do to get him in?"

"I'm afraid not. He has on jeans and a t-shirt with tennis shoes."

Brown chuckles, "Okay, I'm on my way out. Can you get my check please!"

"Yes Sir."

Moments later Brown approaches Octavius standing out front. Octavius disappointed, "Dude, I didn't know this was a five-star restaurant."

Brown nonchalantly, "No biggie! Let's just go across the street to the pizza parlor."

"NO! Let's dine here. I've never been in a five-star steak house."

"Your attire is not up to par."

"I tried to tell dude I had shoes and a shirt in the car."

Brown's facial expression changed, "Is that right?"

"I told the dude at the door. He just told me step to the side."

"Go ahead and change! I'll meet you inside."

Brown could be seen talking with someone at the front desk while Octavius went to change. Octavius returns to the restaurant. His jacket was too short and too tight. Brown chuckles when the waiter escorts Octavius back to his table. The waiter was obviously upset that Octavius was allowed to dine. Brown with a very stern voice, "Thank you!"

Octavius with the biggest grin nods in the waiter's direction. Octavius slides down into his seat taking in the sites. "Dude, so this how you living?" Octavius asked.

Brown unfazed by the remarks just strolls through his phone. He glances at Octavius, "I took the liberty of ordering for you." Octavius eyes buck when he sees the menu and prices. "I ordered the Kobe beef and lobster tail with potato au gratin and house wine."

Octavius' eyes peer over in the corner of the menu where that meal is located at $175 per person. *Instantly he thinks back to one of his old high school friends who went to lunch with someone she just met. The date was great until the guy skipped out on the check. The restaurant called the police, and she had to make arrangements to pay or go to jail for a $350 meal.* At that moment Octavius questions Brown, "So what is it you want to talk about? I'm not really that hungry."

A split second later the waiter is setting their food on the table. Brown glances at Octavius, "Bon Appetite!"

Octavius digs in cutting a small piece of the Kobe steak, "Just so you know I don't do dishes."

Browns smirks watching Octavius enjoy their meal. Thirty minutes has passed with small talk. Brown says to Octavius, "I'm not sure if you know, but there's plenty money to be made in your line of work."

Octavius' eyebrows rise slightly, "I'm listening."

Brown leans forward to whisper, "Let's just say I have a 'can't fail' system on the worldwide web."

Octavius smirks wiping his mouth, "That's what Numb Nuts told me when I started working for him at Computer Zone. They're clearing $20,000 a month at that location. Just think they own 25 stores worldwide."

"That's nothing compared to what we can do, if you help me out with my latest project?"

"You have my interest," Octavius replies. Brown goes into detail about his plan. Octavius chuckles once Brown is done talking, "Have you lost your mind? That's crazy!"

Brown offended challenges Octavius, "Is that all you are is a yes man to Computer Zone? Do you have any balls at all? You would love to be in my shoes, right?"

The waiter walks over passing the check to Brown who declines, "No, give the check to that gentleman."

Octavius' greatest fear comes to life. He starts to sweat lightly. Brown recognizes the fear in Octavius facial expression when he glances at the tab. "Where are my manners? I invited you out. Pass that over here."

Octavius swallows his pride, "Really Dude! Three hundred dollars for dinner? You must be ball'in?" Octavius goes into geek mode calculating in his mind, 300 x 7 = 2100, and there are four weeks in a month which gives you $8400 on food.

The waiter returns to the table with Brown's credit card. "Thank you, Mr. Tate. Will you be taking anything with you?"

Octavius confused. "Tate?"

Brown smirks and responds quickly to the waiter, "No! Have the valet pull my car around please."

"Yes, Mr. Tate," the waiter replies.

Octavius with the biggest grin ever, "So who are you again?"

Brown whispers, "I'm nobody and everybody at the same time."

Octavius ponders on Brown's words speaking out loud, "I'm nobody and everybody at the same time. Well said, Mr. Brown or Tate, if you want to confuse people."

Outside waiting for the valet, "Thanks for the extravagant dinner."

The valet pulls up in a late model Mercedes Benz coupe all black everything, tinted windows and black rims. "You're welcome!"

Brown pulls out a wad of cash to tip the valet. Octavius could not help but notice all the hundred dollar bills. Brown peels off three hundred dollars passing them to Octavius. Octavius reluctant, "No thanks!"

"I insist ... here take it. Go find that girl from the store and take her to dinner."

Octavius with a big grin, "Yes ... Yes ... Yes ... that's my type of girl. However, I'm not her type of guy."

Brown with a slight giggle sits inside his Mercedes, "If you have money, you are all women's type."

Octavius nods in agreement extending his hand for the cash, "Okay, I'll buy that. Did you see the breast on that girl from the store? Cassie. They were so perky, and she smelled so good. You think those were natural or implants?"

"They were natural."

"How do you know that?"

"They had a slight sag and bounce to them and implants don't move that well."

Octavius jokingly, "What are you some type of boob doctor or something?"

Brown pulls away slowly. Octavius admires the car speaking out loud with a goofy laugh. "Thanks, Brown, or whoever you are!"

It's a sunny day and Octavius rides his hoverboard to work. Mr. Fisher gives Octavius a hard stare, "So, you're just going to continue to come in here late?"

Octavius looks up at the clock. "Dude, it's 9:05! I'm five minutes late! Get off my back will you!"

Octavius removes his backpack walking into the back room. Octavius returns back into the store with his headphones rocking back and forth. Mr. Fisher is getting upset because he can hear Octavius' music. Octavius takes a seat at his workstation pulling out a laptop. He stops rocking to the music. He senses someone standing over him. He leans back peering over his shoulder, and Mr. Fisher is standing there. He removes one side of his headphones, "WHAT NOW?!"

"That music is too loud. Customers don't want to hear that when they come in the store. Turn it off!" Mr. Fisher demanded.

Octavius lets out a deep breath in frustration. "You cool now?"

"No! Have you started on the young lady's website?" Octavius quickly boots up his computer going to Cassie's website. Stanley Fisher stands behind him looking on. Cassie is in a split pose, topless covering her nipples with two fingers from each hand.

"Ooo Lala…." Stanley Fisher says.

"Dude, move back!"

The door chimes indicating that a customer has entered the store. "I want to see more after I take care of this customer," Mr. Fisher states.

"Yeah ... whatever! This ain't that!" Octavius replies and logs on to Cassie's site.

Mr. Fisher proceeds to assist the customer talking loudly to Octavius. "You're going to find yourself without a job one of these good ole days." Octavius glances at Mr. Fisher placing his headphones back on. Mr. Fisher just keeps threatening Octavius' job.

At the end of the day, Octavius grabs his backpack and exits without uttering a word. "No one person is bigger than the company. Everyone is expendable!" says Mr. Fisher.

Octavius just continues to walk out the door placing his hoverboard on the ground. He steps aboard riding off. Mr. Fisher angry, "I hope it blows up! That way I won't have to fire your ass."

Octavius arrives back at his West Loop apartment that is being renovated. He picks up his hoverboard walking inside the lobby. The building manager meets him in the lobby in his business attire, "Hey Octavius!"

"How's it going, Mr. Stagni?"

"Construction is going well. It's only a matter of time before we reach your floor. I only hope that you are prepared to take one of the lower floors or move."

"Well, the rent has doubled on the renovated floors. Is there any discount for existing tenants, Mr. Stagni?"

"Unfortunately, no, the area has changed drastically. It's only a matter of time before this area is considered upper to middle class."

Octavius' mood changes instantly, feeling bummed out, "Yep I have noticed."

Mr. Stagni adjusts his Chopard® wristwatch, "You have maybe another week before they're knocking on your door."

"Yeah ... I know. Have a good evening, Sir." Mr. Stagni turns away from Octavius speaking to the doorman. Octavius steps into the elevator. *"Damn! What the fuck! I can't catch a break,"* speaking to himself. He walks into his apartment falling onto his couch in disbelief.

Downtown ... Cassie's on a blind date eating dinner with a gentleman that her girlfriend, Khloe, set up. Brad is the athletic type, low haircut, wearing Levi's jeans and a T-shirt. Cassie sits there and listens to Brad talk about his business. She sits looking like a supermodel as Brad continues.

"So, Brad, how do you think we are looking on a second date?"

Brad pauses, "I think we are good for a few dates."

"Really?"

"Why? Do you not like this restaurant?"

Cassie annoyed, "No, the restaurant is fine. It's your ass I could do without."

Brad stunted, "What ... what did I do wrong?"

Cassie stands grabbing her designer Prada bag, "Everything!" She turns and walks away from the table leaving Brad speechless. Cassie, on her way out the door, grabs her cell phone from her bag. She calls Khloe.

"Hey Cassie! How's your date? Brad is one fine guy."

"Yeah, that would be true, if you like conceited assholes!"

Khloe laughs, "Girl, you're stupid."

"The entire time I was there all he did was talk about himself. Hell, I felt like I was interviewing him for a job."

"Girl, you know that you can be silly. Damn! Was it that bad?"

"Damn what?" Cassie asks.

"Girl, you know Brad owns a few party buses. I was thinking about renting one for my birthday."

"Hell, Khloe, you should have told me that shit. He's not bad looking or anything, but he is a lame."

Khloe laughs, "How is he a lame? He has his own everything. You're tweakin', Girl."

Cassie looks down at her phone, and it's Brad calling. "Girl, it's Brad calling on my other line. I told you he was a lame. How in the hell does someone walk out on you and you call them back?"

Khloe pauses, "Yep, you're right. Lame!" They both crack up laughing.

"Khloe, I'm gone, and the next time you want to hook me up, do me a favor ... DON'T! Bye! I have to order an Uber."

Khloe laughs, "Good bye, Crazy!"

Cassie is riding in the back of the Uber cab. She pulls out her lip liner and a mirror. She touches up her lips with the liner and applies some lip gloss. She takes several selfies. She strolls through the selfies with a bright smile, "*Now that's what's up!*"

Octavius is sitting on his couch in deep thought. He's debating on whether or not to call Brown. He picks up his cell phone to dial. He starts to pace back and forth around the apartment, "What the hell am I getting into?" He looks down at Brown's number on the screen. He is just about to hit the call button, "*No...No...No...No...,*" stopping the call. He continues to talk out loud, "*If you don't do this ... where will you go? I could go to my grandma's house, but it's too many people there. I need my own space. I need a raise in pay. I need a new car, and hell, a new life. Look at this place.*" He surveys his apartment then pushes the call button. The phone just rings, "*Come on ... pick up the phone.*"

"Hello!"

Octavius with excitement in his voice, "Hey Dude! What's crack'in?"

Brown very mild manner, "Life! What's happening in your world?"

"Not much, but I decided that I want to check out what we talked about."

Brown curious, "Why the sudden change? You seemed very reluctant before?"

At that moment Octavius looks in the mirror and did not like the reflection. "Brown, life happens."

Brown chuckles, "Okay then. Text me your address and I come by and pick you up tomorrow. Know this, to play the part you have to look the part." Octavius hunches his shoulders looking in the mirror, *"Whatever that means."* "Right, see you tomorrow around 10 am," Brown replies.

"I have to work tomorrow," Octavius responds. Brown didn't say a word. He just listens to Octavius. *"Hello...Hello? Damn! These cell phones are crazy."* Octavius speaks out loud. Brown smirks ending the call.

The next day Octavius is up ready and waiting. His cell phone just keeps ringing. He looks at the caller ID. It's Mr. Fisher. His text alert chirps. The message is from Mr. Fisher, "I DARE YOU NOT ANSWER, YOU LITTLE SHIT. IF YOU'RE NOT HERE IN THE NEXT HOUR, YOU NO LONGER HAVE A JOB!"

Octavius shakes his head before texting back, "Look here, Dad's girl, you don't know anything about computers or anything else for that matter! SCREW YOU, DUDE!" Octavius is about to press the send button and decides to press delete message. He doesn't respond to Mr. Fisher's text. His cell phone rings showing anonymous. He hesitates before answering in a soft whisper voice, "Hello?"

Brown yells, "HELLO! I'm downstairs, Dude, come on out."

Octavius gathers his things quickly, "I'm coming right down." He steps off the elevator and sees Cassie waiting. "Wow! What a surprise seeing you here?"

Cassie gives him the cold shoulder. "Nice to see you too, Octavius. Meet my friend, Chad." She turns to explain to Chad how she met Octavius. Before Cassie could finish the introduction Octavius walks away. Cassie turns to Chad, "Now that was odd." Cassie and Chad enter the elevator.

Octavius steps out of the building on this very sunny day pulls out his geek like sunglasses, and makes his way over to Brown's late model Mercedes AMG CL550. Brown laughs when Octavius opens the door. Octavius trying to play the part sits down and puts on his seat belt. Brown pulls away swiftly making the exhaust roar loudly. They cruise down Michigan Avenue as Octavius stares out at all the people walking around. He snaps out of his daze when his cell phone vibrates, checking the call ... it's Mr. Fisher.

"Damn!" Octavius mumbles.

"Dude, what's going on?" Brown asks.

Looking at his phone, "It's Fish Head."

"Your boss?" Brown asks.

"Yep, that be the one I call Fish Head!"

Brown giggles, "Man, screw Fish Head. We're about to get money, my Dude." Brown turns up in Macy's parking lot. "Let's do some shopping that will make you feel better."

"Not really. I don't have any money for anything out of Macy's."

"Don't worry about it. They have plenty sample packages of cologne. Besides this will be the best day of your life," Brown states. They ride the escalator up to the first floor and immediately start shopping.

Brown takes Octavius over to the watch counter. The salesperson walks up as Octavius looks at the prices. "Damn! These watches are expensive. I never even heard of Chopard."

The salesperson slides open the display case removing the watch that caught Octavius' eye. She opens the band reaching for Octavius wrist. "This one is a Chopard® Gran Turismo. The band is made from recycled Gran Turismo tire tread from the race track. It's a Swiss watch with 18 Karat white gold housing." She fastens the band on his wrist. Octavius admires the watch.

"How much for this watch, Ma'am?" Octavius asks.

She looks on the tag on the back of the box, "This one is $8,500, but it's on sale for $6,500 today."

Octavius' eyes buck, "That's kind of steep." He starts to remove the watch.

Brown starts laughing, "Dude, you only live once. To play the part you have to look the part."

Octavius slightly disappointed, "Yeah ... yeah."

"We'll take it," Brown says.

Octavius confused and excited at the same time, "Thanks, Dude!"

"And how will you be paying today, cash or charge?"

"Charge," Brown passing over his credit card and identification. His cell phone rings. The name Ivan appears on his screen. He sends the call to voice mail.

The salesperson returns with the box and receipt, "Here you go, Mr. Matthews. I need your signature at the bottom of the receipt."

Brown signs the receipt. Octavius zones out, "*I can sale this watch and get at least half price.*"

"Dude, let's go." Brown states. Octavius walks quickly. Brown laughs, "Dude, slow down. You act like you stole something."

Octavius, a nervous wreck, "I never did anything remotely close to this." They head back down the escalator to the shoe area. Brown is looking at some Gucci loafers with the Gucci buckle on top. Octavius picks up the shoe to look at the price. His mouth hangs open, "Damn, Brown, $2,200 for some shoes? What they do? Walk by themselves?"

Brown chuckles, "Man, you're a funny Dude. Let's get out of here." They walk to the exit.

Back at the newly renovated condos Cassie is doing a photoshoot. Chad has all the equipment set up in the living room. Cassie's place is very nicely decorated and bright. Chad goes over to close the blinds setting the lighting in the room. He walks the room with his light meter. Cassie comes out wearing a robe with flawless makeup.

Chad nods in approval, "That's a hot look on you. Hold it right there. Let me grab the camera." He removes the cap from the lens and starts to give orders. "I'm going to need you to remove that robe ever so slowly." Cassie reveals her shoulder and slowly slides her arm out of the robe.

"Hold that pose right there. Nice. Tilt your head slightly and smile without showing any teeth. Okay, nice," Chad keeps taking pictures. Cassie leans back letting her hair hang and dropping the robe completely. She has on a one-piece black swimsuit with two inch straps covering her private parts. Chad pauses for a second taking in her beauty. Her mulatto skin is radiant with silky black hair and curvy shape. "DAMN! Jeans don't do you any justice hiding that body of yours," Chad says.

"Whatever! I know you have seen better bodies than mine," Cassie replies.

Chad continues to take pictures. "Okay, I need for you to put on some heels, preferably red."

"Okay," Cassie strolls away. Chad adjusts his crouch in his pants to get some comfort from the erection he got watching Cassie.

Moments later, Cassie comes out wearing red heels and red lipstick to match. Chad watches her ass, poking out from those four inch heels. Chad goes over to dim the light. He knocks one over on Cassie's table. "HEY! Be careful," Cassie shouts.

"My fault," Chad grabs a wooden chair and spins it in Cassie's direction. "Have a seat with your thighs facing the back of the chair." Cassie takes a seat. "Sit up straight and cross your arms on the back of the chair." Cassie does it cracking her neck to loosen up. Chad immediately picks up the camera, starts shooting and giving more orders.

"Teeth … smile … I need teeth! Okay, stand and turn around with your arms on the back of the chair bent over," Chad demands. Cassie getting into her groove moves on command. Chad getting worked up, "Open up those legs! There should be no thighs touching."

Cassie widens up her stand, "Like this?"

"No, I still see thighs touching."

"How about now? Is this good enough?"

Chad walks over to position Cassie sticking his hand between Cassie's thighs tipping them for more space to open up. He takes a deep breath smelling her perfume. He tries to regain his composer.

"Okay, now slide your top piece down to where the bikini part starts." Cassie removes her arms sliding down the top part exposing her firm breast. Chad starts to turn and a drop of sweat forms on his forehead. He walks over grabs the camera trying to focus. "Okay! Look back at it, Girl!"

Cassie looks back at her ass. Chad continues to take pictures. "Okay, that's it, Chick!"

Cassie frowns, "No, I want to take one more."

"How so?"

Cassie starts to remove her swimsuit, "Naked! Every person wants a picture of themselves naked." She straddles the chair and instantly Chad's leg starts rocking. She gives her best sexy pose with both arms over her head. Chad reaches for the camera taking her into view. He starts clicking away staring at her firm C-cups and erect nipples. She switches the pose crossing her legs leaning forward with her face close to the camera while giving a close up view of her breasts. He lets out a loud grunt, "OH OH ... SHIT!"

Cassie runs over to his aid, "Are you okay?" Chad is sweating profusely and shaking down on one knee. "Chad, are you okay? Should I call for some help?"

He holds still for a moment, "Ooh ooh ... ah ... Woo Girl!"

"Woo Girl, what?" She ponders on the thought of the sounds Chad is making. "I know you didn't just get off watching me? OH HELL NO!" She quickly takes offense to the idea grabbing her robe covering up.

Chad giggles for a second. His only defense is, "I'm a man. It's natural, right?" Cassie burst out laughing loudly. Chad confused, "What's so funny?"

"You're funny as in gay, right?"

Chad annoyed in a very sarcastic manner, "No, Honey, I'm bi-sexual, and I still like fine women."

Cassie ties her robe, "This is too much. You better get cleaned up." She laughs some more.

Over on Michigan Avenue Octavius is getting some pointers from Brown. The streets are packed with business people, homeless, and hustlers. Brown points things out to Octavius before they happen. "Octavius, look over to your left at the girl and guy."

"Yeah, what about them?"

"They're about to steal that lady's identity."

"How do you know that?"

"Just watch." The young girl stops an older woman as if she is lost. She asks for directions while her male friend bumps her purse with some device. The older woman turns to explain by pointing her finger in the direction the young girl should be traveling. The young girl nods and thanks the older woman as she quickly catches up with her male friend.

"I didn't see him go inside her purse."

Brown smirks, "That's the beauty of it. You know longer have to go inside their purse with the latest technology. Everybody wants to store information in their phone."

Octavius disagrees, "No, it's easier to steal a wallet then to crack somebody's security code." Brown shakes his head as they keep walking. Octavius glances down at his new watch for the time, "Where to now?"

Brown keeps walking, "Home. I'm going to drop you off at home now."

Octavius nods, "Cool." In the car on the way back to his apartment, the music is playing. Octavius has his own little vibe going grooving to the beat. His phone vibrates interrupting his vibe. He looks at the screen it's Mr. Fisher. His demeanor changes instantly. Brown chuckles to himself. "Brown, can you drop me off at work?" Octavius asks.

"No problem. I thought we just left work. That watch is worth more than you make in a week or month."

"Yeah it is, but I can't pay bills with it."

"You can do with it as you wish. It belongs to you."

Octavius looks down at the watch admiring the design, "Nope, I'm going to keep this one." They pull up in front of Octavius' job. He opens the door, "Okay, B, I'll talk with you later."

Brown nods in disapproval, "Yeah okay, Oh. I'll give you a call later."

Octavius closes the door and all you hear are the roar of the pipes which catches Mr. Fisher's ear. From inside the store you can see Mr. Fisher trying to see who got out of the car. Octavius strolls into the store. Mr. Fisher can't help but to snap on Octavius. "YOU HAVE GOT TO BE KIDDING ME! You walk up in her all nonchalant like you run the place. You're over three hours late. I saw you get out of that fancy car with your new buddy."

Octavius stands his ground staring at Mr. Fisher, "Are you done yet?"

Mr. Fisher is furious, "One of these good ole days...."

Octavius gives a silly grin, "One of these days what?" Mr. Fisher stands in silence. "That's what I thought. Now I'm going to get to work if you don't mind!" Octavius stares at Fisher while flexing his new watch.

"Oh Yeah, it's like that huh?" Mr. Fisher asks.

"Yep! Just like that!" The stare down continues while Octavius walks over to his station. Octavius takes a seat while celebrating under his breath. *"I'm the man."*

*   *   *

A few days later, one late evening, Brown goes to meet Ivan. Ivan is the manager at a five-star hotel downtown. Ivan and Brown have come up with a system that is fool proof. Ivan gets the credit card numbers and sells them to Brown. Brown takes the credit card numbers, keep the corporate accounts, and sells the others to low level hustlers. Brown rolls up in front of Ivan's job. Brown calls inside, "I'm out here."

"Fo Sho that brother," Ivan replies.

Moments later, Ivan comes tiptoeing out to the car as if it is some important person. Brown laughs as Ivan gets in the car. "Look at you with your vest and bow tie."

Ivan unamused, "Look, man, this is serious business."

"I'm just complimenting you on your attire. No harm in that right?" Brown laughs.

"Yo, man, real talk. I'm going to have to charge you double for these numbers."

Brown's facial expression changes from joking to serious. "What are you saying?"

"What did I just say ... double! Like ten grand ... double."

Brown hesitates, "So you're getting greedy now? Five grand isn't enough?"

Ivan puts both hands up, "Pump the brakes, Playa. What I'm saying is corporate has been breathing down my back about some identity theft ring in Chicago. If I'm going to continue to take this risk, I need to be compensated. I'm saying this could cost me my job, if I get caught and it has to be worth it to me."

"Okay, I respect your position now and where you're coming from. In that case, no problem. I'll just have to tax the guys on the back end."

Ivan's eyes lit up with a big grin, "See that's what I'm talking about. I knew you would understand."

Brown leans against the driver's door. "Do you have the black box with you?"

"Do you have the cash?" Ivan asks.

"I don't come empty-handed ever do I?" Brown reaches under the seat.

Ivan panics, "HOLD UP, PLAYA. What you reaching for?"

Brown smirks, "Your money." He pulls up $5000 in hundreds.

Ivan goes in his pocket pulling out the credit card reader. "It's full 100 numbers as usual."

Brown frowns, "It better be. I know where you work." Brown bursts out laughing.

"Damn, B, you're always on some bullshit. I wasn't scared just so you know. I'm out. Gotta get back to the plantation."

"You're a fool with it! Later, Dude." Brown says. Ivan jogs back to work as Brown cruises off in deep thought. *This Chump trippin' if he thinks I'm going to pay him ten grand.*

A few days passed and Brown is at his condo sitting watching his computer screen. He's trying to find a way to break this encryption code. He taps on the computer keyboard rather quickly several times without any luck. He gets frustrated flipping over the keyboard in anger. He looks at his reflection in the computer monitors, *Octavius can break this code.* Brown starts to rock back and forth in his computer chair. He grabs his cell phone to call Octavius. Octavius is at home working on his latest project of piracy. He's hacking into major record labels files and releasing their files for free. Octavius giggles as his virus eats up the firewall looking for an opening. His cell phone rings. He answers with a hint of excitement in his voice, "What's crackin', B?"

Brown stern and very serious, "It's time, Octavius."

"For what?"

"To take this game to the next level. Are you with it?"

"That's funny because I'm watching my virus eat up this firewall like a Pac Man game looking for power pellets," Octavius giggles.

"I'll let you get back to that small thing you call fun. I'm going to text you my address so you can come over tonight."

Octavius looks down at his watch, "It's 8:00 already, Man."

"Do you have a curfew?"

"Nope!"

"Take Uber or Lyft to my place now."

"On my way. Money calls, right? Should I bring my laptop?"

"If you'd like!" Octavius looks at his computer screen wondering how much longer before he'd be inside the record company's files. At that very moment the firewall clasps. *"I'm in now,"* with a big devilish grin on his face typing quickly on the keypad. Moving his mouse over to unreleased new artists and downloading all the files to the internet for free. He clicks on one of the new artist's songs. It's a young lady who is very attractive. He waits for the music to begin as he packs up to leave. He nods in approval looking back at the screen tossing his backpack over his shoulder. He giggles while looking at his signature bird fly back across the screen stealing the record company's files.

In the lobby, Cassie is waiting on the elevator while talking to Khloe. The bell chimes for the opening of the elevator doors. A couple of people step out before Octavius. Cassie smiles when she sees Octavius. "Hey, Octavius!"

Octavius with a stern look gives her the head nod and keeps it moving. Cassie steps into the elevator talking to Khloe. "Girl, I just saw the geek, and he didn't even speak."

"Well, maybe your geek is more like a creep."

"Whatever!" The elevator doors close.

Octavius is standing at the counter waiting to be announced. The doorman calls up to the apartment, "Mr. Brown, you have an Octavius here to see you. Okay, Sir, he's on his way up. Sir, please sign in for me right here, and it's the door to your left apartment 1940."

Octavius signs, "Thanks!"

Before Octavius could knock on the door Brown pulls it open. "What's up, my Dude?"

Octavius gazes over the apartment in amazement, "Damn, Dude, this is one lavish pad you got here. I did some work for Fish Head over here for some millionaire cat in the penthouse."

Brown, not impressed, "There are some pretty wealthy people up in this building."

"Damn, Dawg! This is really nice."

"So you think?" Brown asks.

"Yes, Sir! I know this is that life I was born to live. Fish Head lives pretty well off all my hard work."

Brown concerned, "You didn't strike me as the type to trip about other people's success. Did I miss something?"

"No, it just irritates the hell out of me when Fisher starts bragging about what he has acquired. When for real he hasn't done anything on his own. He's a trust fund baby."

Brown very smooth and convincing walks over to the living room windows pulling the curtains back while speaking. "I'll get for you what is due to you only if you trust me to set it up for you? Think of the world as a sandbox to play in."

Octavius looking at the city skyline, "This is what I call the High Life!"

Brown chuckles, "No, this my life, but it can be yours if you want it." In an instant Octavius replays his financial problems, *my bills due, about to be homeless, I can't afford the new rent, my boss is a jerk and I'm single.* He rubs his hand over his eyes to keep tears back looking at the Magnificent Mile under his feet. Brown plays on the desperation in Octavius' facial expression, walks over, places his hand on his shoulder. "All of your financial problems are about to end. Come with me!"

"Where are we going?"

They exit the apartment going around the corner to another apartment. Octavius glancing at the apartment number while Brown opens the door. They enter, and Octavius makes a quick observation, *"Under furnished, but clean."*

"Come into this room," Brown says. Octavius' face lights up immediately. The room is full of office furniture, new computers and monitors. The monitors have some financial transactions taking place. "Have a seat," Brown says.

Octavius sits behind the desk, "Why is the system moving so fast?"

Brown ponders for a second thinking if Octavius is the guy for the job. "This system tracks financial institutions and online banking systems."

Octavius intrigued, "Okay…. So what do you need me to do?"

"I've been monitoring accounts with no activity. These systems that move quickly are impossible to monitor; however, these systems that aren't moving like the three in the corner." He points to those accounts.

"Okay, I see them."

"I think we can move those funds." Octavius' heart pounds in his chest with thought of what Brown is asking him to do. However, the excitement of cracking into corporate America's financial market is more exhilarating. Brown stands over Octavius. "So what are you thinking?"

"I think it can be done, but it's going to take some time."

Brown smirks opening up the desk drawer. He reaches inside pulling out a stack of one hundred dollar bills totaling $5,000. "Here's a little something to hold you over until we can crack these accounts."

Octavius turns, looks at the cash slowly reaching for it. He grabs it never holding five grand before he gets nervous. Brown smirks with sure delight knowing that Octavius is on the job and it will only be a matter of time before he figures out the system. "Oh yeah, it's time to live the American dream."

Octavius confused, "What dream might that be?"

"Fine women, fast cars, and fast money that's your dream, right?"

"Kind of ... sort of.... I really want Cassie. She's perfect for me."

"The young lady from the computer store wearing the swimsuit?"

"Yes, Sir!"

"She'll be chasing you before it's all over. Here are two corporate credit cards without limits. Go shopping tomorrow and buy everything you ever thought you might want. You have to look the part though. As a matter of fact, why don't you come by tomorrow around 10:00 am and pick up the Benz. You can keep it for a couple of days. I'm going out of town."

Octavius blown away by the opportunity, "Yeah ... okay."

"We are partners so we share things."

Octavius nods his head frantically in agreement, "Yep partners."

Back over at Cassie's apartment she has the phone on speaker talking to Khloe. "Girl, did I tell you about your boy Chad?"

"MY BOY! The photographer?"

"Yes! OMG, GIRL! I didn't know that he was bi-sexual. Home boy must have gotten his rocks off at the photo shoot."

Khloe bursts out laughing, "No he didn't. You're a liar."

"May the devil himself come and get me if I'm lying."

Khloe silent for a moment, "Do you think that's his method of getting women?"

"Hell to the no! He's gay for sure with his prissy ass."

"Girl that's too funny." Khloe continues to laugh.

"Girl, hold on a minute. The Geek is calling."

"Girl, you've got too many problems with men."

Cassie switches over to the other line. "Hello!"

"Hey, Cassie! This is Octavius."

Cassie, with an attitude, "Okay, and?"

"I had a chance to look over the photos you emailed to me. You look very nice. However, those outfits look kind of outdated."

Cassie offended, "Whatever do you mean? That is designer swimwear and jeans. You tweaking."

Octavius giggles, "Outdated designer swimwear and jeans like I said."

Cassie changes the subject, "Have you completed my website?"

"No, you need new gear."

"I don't have money for that right now. So unless you are buying, use what I sent to you."

"I have no problem buying for you. That's why I'm calling. I would like to take you shopping for some new gear so you can have the hottest website in town."

Cassie's entire demeanor changes to pleasant, "Town? How about the world?"

Octavius reserves, "Okay, Cassie, I'll see you tomorrow around noon in the lobby." Cassie ends the call sitting on the edge of her bed with a silly grin. Octavius stares at Cassie's picture on her website.

At the Federal building downtown, Ivan is in the interrogation room sitting at the table with his attorney. The U.S. Marshal is present sitting directly across from Ivan's attorney, Ms. Goldstein. Ms. Goldstein, an ex US attorney, has a private practice. They wait patiently on the U.S. prosecutor. Mr. Goodman walks in the room known for his conviction rate of 87 percent on identity theft. Mr. Goodman, well-dressed and groomed, unbuttons his suit coat and takes a seat. "Hello everyone," Mr. Goodman says.

Ms. Goldstein smiles, "Hello, Ronald."

Mr. Goodman with the most serious look clears his throat. "Now let me be straight forward here, Ms. Goldstein. Your client was in possession of several fraudulent credit cards, not to mention a black box credit card reader that stored 100 stolen credit card numbers. How does he wish to proceed?"

"My client does admit to possessing fraudulent credit cards, however, the black box was not in his possession. I also requested a copy of the arrest warrant, which has not yet been provided," Ms. Goldstein responds.

"I'm sure that we can get you a copy of the arrest warrant. I take it that your client intends to take this case further?" Mr. Goodman asks.

"My client would like to see all the evidence against him before so that he can make an informed decision."

"I usually don't operate this way, but for the sake of time I'll divulge something. On this date, Ivan Smith was observed getting out of a late model Mercedes while he was at work." Ivan taps his attorney's leg under the table. She glances down at her notepad writing on it. *LET THEM TALK!* "Moreover, on that same night undercover officer, Mackie, retrieved torn up documents from your client's trash. Those documents were linked to your client's job with more stolen numbers," Mr. Goodman states.

Ivan begins rocking back and forth in his chair. Ms. Goldstein turns her chair in Ivan's direction she whispers to Ivan, "So how do you wish to proceed?"

Ivan cocky, "I'm sticking to the G code. Besides this is the preliminary, and they really don't have anything on me right?"

"No! They do have something on you," Ms. Goldstein replies.

"Okay, tell them suit up. Game on!" Ivan says.

"Okay." She swings her chair back around facing Mr. Goodman.

Mr. Goodman veers out of the United States Sentencing Guideline book. "So has your client decided?" Mr. Goodman asks.

"Yes, my client would like to move forward in U.S. vs. Ivan Smith," Ms. Goldstein responds shaking her head in disbelief.

"Okay, in this case of U.S. vs. Ivan Smith, this case carries a minimum sentence of 96 months and maximum of 144 months," Mr. Goodman states.

"Okay, when is the next hearing? I'm trying to bond out of here."

"Only a cash bond will be accepted in this matter in the amount of $50,000," Mr. Goodman says with a smirk.

Ivan's calculating the math in his head trying to convert the months into years. It comes to him, eight to 12 years. Ivan is about to be removed from the prosecutor's office. The U.S. Marshals approach Ivan. At that moment he faints falling to the floor.

"Get a medic in here immediately," Mr. Goodman giggles. "Do it like a G, huh?"

The other officers chuckle as they help Mr. Ivan Smith back in his chair. Ms. Goldstein just stares at Ivan as he tries to regain consciousness shaking her head.

That evening Brown was in Virginia meeting with some technology guy. They had only met over the internet. Brown waiting in this upscale sports bar sips on an ice cold beer out of a frosted mug. He pulls out his cell phone to text Alex. He starts his text to Alex, and a shadow looms over him from behind. He turns to see this six foot five, 300-pound guy standing over him. The big guy steps to the side, and Alex steps out of the shadow extending his hand to Brown. The big guy, Mason, sits across the room as Brown and Alex talk business.

Alex, a frail, mid-30s, white guy, speaks with confidence. "This technology hasn't hit the market, and I'm not really sure if it will." Brown listens intensely while gulping his beer. Alex continues to speak as the waitress approaches.

"Hello, Gentlemen. May I take your order please!" the waitress asks. The waitress' beauty catches Brown off guard when he glances up. He quickly regains his composer turning his attention back to Alex.

"I'll have the Beer Batter Chicken Tenders with Fries," Alex says. "Anything for you, my friend?" Alex asks.

"No thanks," Brown replies.

"Okay, Sir, I'll put your order in," the waitress says turning to walk away. Alex and Brown both watch the young lady as she walks away.

"That's one hot chick," Alex states. Brown nods in agreement. "Anyhow, there are a few prototypes out here of this state of the art card reader. The beauty in this is that it's micro thin. You can just clip it onto any card reader anywhere to choose what cards you want and dispose the numbers you don't. Here's the ticker … this can all be done from your phone."

Brown impressed but not convinced, "How do I know that this technology works?"

Alex smiles looking at Mason with a simple head nod. Mason gets up, walks over to the jukebox sliding a plastic clip inside the card reader. He stands there looking over the music playlist then returns to his seat. Once Mason makes it back to his seat he gives Alex a head nod. Alex quickly turns his phone in Brown's direction so that he can see the screen. Alex navigates to his app that flashes ready.

"Here you go, Sir," the waitress puts the food down on the table. Brown watches the screen on Alex's phone. "Sir, have you decided on anything?"

Brown gives the waitress a nasty look, "I said no before!"

"My friend, relax. She's just doing her job and a pretty good one at that," Alex states. Mason nods again at Alex indicating that someone is about to use the jukebox. Alex grabs one of the chicken tenders, "Pay attention."

Brown glances at the jukebox while watching the screen on Alex's phone at the same time. The customer inserts his credit card and before he can select the music, his information appears on Alex's phone, PIN number and name. Alex screenshots the information and stores it to his phone.

Brown quite impressed with a smile on his face, "Now I'm ready to eat." He reaches over grabbing one of Alex's chicken tenders. "Not bad."

Alex smirks, "Which one, the app or the chicken?"

"Both. When can I get the card reader and app?"

"How soon can you get the money? I want cash."

"By the end of next week."

"100K by the end of next week, and it's Thursday?"

Brown looks directly in Alex's eyes, "Yes, 100K cash." Alex reaches over the kiosk to pay the tab. He looks as Brown clicks the pay button on his phone and instantly the bill is paid with the information he just stored in his phone.

"Wow! I'm impressed!" Brown says.

Alex extends his hand as he gets up from the table, "I hope to hear from you soon, Brown." Brown quickly gets up leaving the bar very enthusiastically about what he has just witnessed.

The next day Octavius is up bright and early. He's watching the news, "Good news for Illinois Lottery players! Finally, a jackpot winner here in Chicago! The prize of $197 million was purchased on the south side! More information will be provided on the lottery later in the broadcast. Today's weather forecast high in the 70s and sunny."

Octavius grabs the remote turning off the television. He glances at his watch as he heads out the door. Octavius quickly flags down a cab in the West Loop.

"Where to?" the driver asks with a foreign accent.

"Madison and Halsted, Precision Cutz."

"I'm familiar with that barbershop. A lot of celebrities go there. Oh, you must be someone important? They go by appointment only."

"Really?" Octavius speaks to his phone, "Precision Cutz, Chicago." The website appears, and Octavius starts navigating around their website. He's inside the system and is booking an appointment. The cab pulls up in front of the shop.

"That will be $17 dollars, My Friend," the driver states.

Octavius goes inside his pocket pulling out $20. "Thanks, Sir, and keep the change."

Once inside, the receptionist greets Octavius, "Hello, Young Man. Do you have an appointment?"

"Yes!"

"And with whom is your appointment with?"

Octavius scrambling for an answer, "Who's the guy that cuts the Mohawk?"

"You're talking about Tommy. Your name is?"

"Octavius."

The receptionist checks for the appointment as Octavius moves some appointments around from his cell phone. "Sorry, Sir, I don't see your name in here. Could it be with someone else?"

"No, it's with Tommy. Can you check again please?"

"Oh my goodness, it's right here in my face. Don't know what I could have been looking at. Have a seat, Sir, and Tommy will be right with you."

"Thanks!" Octavius smirks.

Tommy walks out to get one of the Bulls players for a cut. "Come on 6'9."

"Excuse me Tommy! This gentleman right here is next on your appointment schedule," the receptionist says.

Tommy confused, "No, 6'9 is here every Friday at 9:45."

The receptionist with an attitude, "Not according to the schedule."

Tommy walks over looks at the screen, "Okay, Young Fella, you're up."

Six-nine slightly upset, "Tommy, Dude, this is some bull!"

"I agree, and that's who you play for the Bull Shitters!!!"

Six-nine laughs it off, "Bro, you got me next right?"

"Yep!"

"That was a good Tommy. You kind of quick with the comebacks." Six-nine said.

"Yep! Something the Bulls haven't done since Mike left the building, come back! Can you hear me now?" The shop erupts in laughter.

"Good one Dude ... good one," while laughing.

Later that evening Cassie and Octavius have been on a shopping spree. They stop at the Water Tower to eat lunch. Cassie has shopping bags from Neiman Marcus, Saks Fifth Avenue, and Macy's. She's having the time of her life. Cassie admires Octavius' new haircut. Octavius has one hand on the table and the other on his cell phone looking down at the screen. Cassie reaches over and grabs his hand. He looks up with a slight smirk. Cassie concerned that Octavius is not feeling her, "Did I do something wrong?"

"No!"

"What's happening?"

"Nothing, Babe, just checking on some of my old clients from Computer World. I feel kind of bad just bouncing on them like that. Fish Head can't service those clients."

"Oh, Octavius, don't be so emotional. Those people can replace you in a heartbeat."

"You think so?"

"No, but anyhow who needs them. Look at us."

Octavius smiles because Cassie seems to be happy. "Finish up your meal! We need to make one more stop."

"I'm done. Where to next?"

"You haven't even eaten any of your food."

Cassie grabs up the packages and Octavius' hand like a kid in a toy store. "Come on!"

Back in Virginia, Brown is getting ready to fly back to Chicago. He stands at the concourse looking out the window at private jets taking off. "Sir, the plane is boarding," the stewardess says.

Brown snapping out of his daze, "Yes, Ma'am, I'm boarding. Thank you."

He turns to board, and the stewardess whispers to one another, "That's one well-dressed man." Seated in first class Brown sips on his Apple Martini. He's thinking about how to raise a 100K. He smirks at the thought that he already has a 100K put away.

* * *

Over in Chicago, Octavius takes Cassie to Tiffany's to look at some jewelry. Cassie gazes down into the display cases and one of the most expensive pieces in the case catches her eye. At that moment a sales woman walks up, "Hello, my name is Angela. How may I assist you today?"

"Hello!" Cassie responds. Octavius with no hesitation points to the chain Cassie has been staring towards.

The sales lady's eyes buck with a smirk on her face thinking, *Why are they looking at this chain, huh ... there is no way on God's green earth they could afford it,* removing it from the display case. "This is one of our more elegant pieces. It's 24 inches long and sterling silver. It retails at $1,200. However, we do have a promotion today that will save you five percent, if you apply for a Tiffany's credit card. Cassie leans forward, and the saleslady fastens it around her neck. The chain looks stunning around Cassie's neck. She admires the chain in the mirror.

"Wow! I never knew that Tiffany's was so pricey." She leans forward so that the sales lady can remove the chain.

"It does look beautiful around your neck. Maybe you would like to start off with one of our smaller pieces?" she asks with a smirk.

Octavius notices the smirk and is slightly offended by the sales lady's comment. "No, we'll be taking that one right there. Keep it on, Cass. As a matter of fact, give her the matching bracelet too."

The saleslady's mouth hangs open for a second. "Okay, that bracelet is an additional $450. Are you sure?"

"I'm sure just put it on her wrist and tell me my damage!"

"Excuse me, Sir, damage?" the saleslady asks.

"Yeah! That means total where I'm from," Octavius responds.

"Oh, okay. Your total is $1,800.23."

Cassie gives Octavius a nonchalant look, "Babe, we don't have to get it today."

The sales lady's smirk gets even bigger thinking, *I knew they couldn't afford the chain or the bracelet.* Octavius reaches into his pocket pulling out a roll of hundred dollar bills. "What are you some type of rapper?" the saleslady asks.

Octavius giggles slightly, "No, I'm a Rock Star!"

Cassie bursts out laughing, "SHUT UP! You are so crazy, Babe." She hugs Octavius' neck really tight planting a big kiss on his lips. Octavius hands the money to the saleslady.

"You are one special young lady. It took me five years for me to get a gift like this from my husband."

"I know...." Cassie replies. They turn to exit the store, and Cassie asks, "Babe, why didn't you use a credit card?"

Octavius kind of snappy, "Now you are getting in my business! Don't ask questions. The reason I used cash is so you can always bring it back if it somehow gets damaged."

"Okay, no more questions. Thanks!"

Over at Computer World, Mr. Fisher has been interviewing to fill Octavius' position. The store clientele is slowing down. Mr. Fisher sits in the office that faces the main street. He has a great love for sports cars. At that moment a black car pulls up out front. Mr. Fisher mumbles, "Black Mercedes AMG Coupe ... nice!" The hazard lights flash and the driver side door opens. Octavius steps out of the car. Mr. Fisher looks closely to make sure it was Octavius. He rushes down to the counter. Octavius walks in and speaks to a couple clients and walks to the back of the store.

Mr. Fisher humbly, "Hey there, Old Buddy, nice ride."

Octavius unfazed by Fisher's acts of kindness, "What's up, Fish?"

"Not much, are you back to work?" Fisher asks.

"Naw, I just came to pick up a few things" Octavius replies.

"The customers miss you, and business is slowing. How about I give you a raise?"

"Naw, I'm good, but thanks for the offer."

Mr. Fisher desperate to have Octavius, "Okay, I'll pay you a salary of $48,000 a year."

Octavius removes a few things from his workstation and chuckles, "A friend of mines said to me you should not buy a car if you don't at least make that amount of money per year. That's a $100,000 car out front."

Mr. Fisher's kindness turns to anger in a low whisper tone, "Why you little arrogant S.O.B.! I don't know what you are up to with your designer jeans and fancy car, but you can rest assured that the bottom is going to fall out of it."

Octavius pauses, looking back over his shoulder at Fisher, "I used to think that you were something like a hater, but I was wrong. You are a hater!" Octavius laughs and walks out the door.

"DON'T COME BACK ASKING FOR YOUR JOB. IF YOU DO, I'LL PAY YOU MIMUNUM WAGE!" Mr. Fisher yells. All Mr. Fisher could hear was the roar of the pipes from the Benz as Octavius sped off.

Two days later, Octavius and Brown are in the condo with the computers, and Octavius is working on getting his virus to penetrate the banking system. Brown is growing impatient, "What's the hold up?"

"These firewalls are very difficult to break and next to impossible. It could take weeks or months before we penetrate the system."

"Okay, in between times we need numbers. I'll have to give Ivan a call over at the hotel. He wants a little more money, but it's worth it."

"Who?" Octavius asks.

Brown turns to leave the room when he gets a text from Alex. *"How's it coming along with those funds? Are we still on for this coming week?"*

Brown pauses in his tracks to respond, *"There has been a slight delay. I'm going to need at least another week."*

"Okay, Buddy. I only have two machines left, and one of them is reserved for you. However, I won't hold it if another buyer comes along. Sorry, Bud!"

Brown frustrated, *"Yep!"*

Octavius notices the frustration on Brown's face. "You cool, Bro?"

Brown nods okay, "I'm going to see Ivan."

Octavius hunches his shoulders, "Okay, you are going to see Ivan. Who Ivan is I don't' know, but going to see Ivan is what it is." Brown walks out the door.

Octavius continues to navigate through the firewall of another major record label. He chuckles and falls back in his seat laughing. He watches his signature bird fly away with unreleased music.

That evening Brown decides to pay a surprise visit to Ivan's workplace. Brown is sitting inside his Mercedes around the corner from Ivan's job when he sees an unmarked car sitting out front. He sits back and observes before calling Ivan's phone. The phone rings and rings just as he's about to hang up, "Hello!" Brown hesitates not recognizing the voice. "Hello? Hello? I guess whoever that was, Ivan, had the wrong phone number." Brown hears laughter just before he ends the call.

"DAMMIT!" Brown punches the steering wheel with frustration. Moments later, Ivan is being escorted out of the building in handcuffs with two agents. Ivan has his head down with shame. His co-workers just look out the door in disbelief. The agent places Ivan in the back seat of the sedan closing the door. Brown is slightly relieved that Ivan has no way of contacting him. At that moment the unmarked car siren comes on and makes a U-turn coming in Brown's direction. As they approach Brown's vehicle, the siren goes off, and they slow down. They're about to pass right by Brown. Ivan and Brown's eyes lock as Ivan stares out the window at Brown. Brown quickly puts his car in gear and speeds away.

The agent smirks, "Yeah, take a good look around. It's going to be awhile before you see any parts of downtown."

The second agent, "That's not true. He gets a rooftop view from MCC. I mean unless you can help us help you?"

They both laugh. Ivan ponders on what the agents are alluding to smirks looking at the agents through the rearview mirror.

Brown enters the condo to find Octavius still there. Octavius is playing a video game, D.R.O.N.E. He pauses the game. "What's good, Bro?"

Brown is pacing back and forward around the room. "Shit, I told him to tone it down just a little bit, but, no, he wants to be Mister Flamboyant!"

"Bro, what the hell are you talking about?"

"Ivan! He just got picked! You know what? Let's hit the club tonight."

"The club, Dude, what's really going on? You come up in here in panic mode."

Brown rubs his palms together. "Get ready! We're going to Club Nympho."

Octavius excited, "That club really does exist? I thought it was some kind of myth."

At Club Nympho the lines are long and the music can be heard outside. Brown and Octavius pull up in the Benz. The valet opens the door for Brown. Brown steps out the car and buttons his jacket.

Octavius looks at the line, "Bro, we're never going to get in this place."

Brown walks around the car towards the security. The security guard removes the rope to allow them to enter. Octavius pauses for a second when he hears someone in line calling his name. He looks in the line, and Cassie and Khloe are in the line. Octavius signals for them to come up. Brown frowns in disagreement. At the front of the line Cassie and Khloe are stopped by security. Cassie frantic, "We're with them." Cassie and Khloe are dressed very provocatively with six inch heels.

"Is that correct, Mr. Carter?" security asks looking at Brown.

Brown nods yes. They enter the club. The music is pounding. The crowd is turnt up! Octavius starts to bounce to the Techno beat. The lights are flashing. Khloe yells out to Cassie, "It's Crack'in up in here."

"I know right," Cassie responds with excitement.

In the VIP section they order bottles and drink the night away. Brown sits nodding to the beat and sipping. He is a little shook up about Ivan's situation. Two Asian women approach Brown. They're very attractive and move provocatively trying to entice him to the dance floor. Khloe has had her eye on Brown all night. She whispers to Cassie, "What's with Octavius' friend? He's very reserved. Is he gay or something? Those girls are nice looking."

Cassie giggles, "Hell if I know. I hope not because if he is, he scoping out my guy…"

"Your guy, huh? You have got to be freaking drunk. I know you are not claiming that lame," looking in Octavius' direction.

Cassie smiles from ear to ear while sipping on her drink, "So what if I am."

Khloe shakes her head, "Hoe, no! We don't do dark skin wannabes."

Cassie smirks, "Girl, light skinned men have played out in my book. He's a game changer."

Octavius comes and grabs Cassie by the hand leading her to the dance floor. They dance very closely as the music pounds. He grinds against Cassie's ass. She bends over slightly putting it all over Octavius' cock area. Octavius, not backing up from the challenge, works his hips from side to side across her ass. Khloe, a bit jealous, sits and watches sipping on her drink, "*Skank*!"

The next day Brown is walking into the bank with a small duffle bag. Moments later he exits the bank taking a quick look around placing his sunglasses on. He continues to his car.

Octavius is sitting in the condo when the door suddenly opens. Brown enters the condo with his duffle bag. He walks over to the table where Octavius is sitting dumps out the contents. "One hundred thousand dollars, Dude, this is how you make moves."

That moment the toilet flushes and Cassie comes walking out the back. Brown furious, "DUDE! WHAT THE FUCK? No one is to be brought here. Now the condo has been compromised." Brown quickly starts stuffing the cash back into the bag. "I can't believe you."

Octavius knowing he just screwed up majorly tries to explain, "Bro, this my lady. She's cool."

"No, she isn't! She's cool for you! Does she know what we are doing here? DOES SHE?"

Octavius scratches his head, "No. Bro!"

Cassie quickly starts to gather her belongings heading for the door. Brown cuts her off in her tracks. Cassie's face shows signs of fear. "And where the hell do you think you're going?" Brown asks.

Cassie drops her head. Octavius stands, "Bro, she doesn't know anything!"

Brown with conviction in his voice, "For your sake, you had better be right!"

Octavius nods no, "She doesn't know, Bro." Tears start to run down Cassie's face out of fear.

Brown turns to open the door, "I'm going out of town to grab those numbers. We'll finish this when I return." He slams the door on his way out.

Cassie jumps at the sound of the door slamming. Tears stream down her face. Octavius quickly goes to console her wrapping his arms around her. Cassie regains her composure pushing Octavius away from her. "What's going on? You guys are drug dealers? Who walks around with a 100 grand besides drug dealers? Huh, Octavius?"

Octavius' mouth is dry, and he can't speak.

Cassie gets louder, "WHO, OCTAVIUS? Brown looked as if he wanted to kill me. Why, Mr. O?

Octavius takes a deep breath, "I think it's time you leave."

"Just like that, huh? No explanation?" Cassie asks.

Octavius nods yes while scratching his head, speaking in a low voice, "Yeah...."

Cassie starts for the door and pauses. "I guess that I'm the lame one here because I have no clue what's going on. Now with that said LOSE MY MOTHER FUCKING NUMBER, LAME!"

Cassie slams the door behind her. Octavius stands in the middle of the room with both hands on top of his head. "DAMMIT!" He kicks over one of the end tables, walks over to the window, crosses his arms in disbelief, "FUCK!"

At the airport Brown is walking down the concourse to his gate. It's a busy day in the airport. He walks into the restroom, places the small duffle bag inside the trash and walks over to the sink to wash his hands. The bathroom clerk comes in removes the trash bag placing it on his cart. Brown turns to exit the restroom walking over to security check. The clerk rolls on by with the trash as Brown gets searched. Brown clears the security check walking down the concourse to the restroom. The clerk is inside the restroom cleaning when Brown walks in. Brown steps over to the sink to look himself over, but really he was checking the restroom. The clerk eases over close to Brown placing the small duffle bag on the sink. Brown places the small duffle bag under his armpit. He removes five crisp hundred dollar bills from his pocket, grabs a paper towel to dry his hands, balling up the money inside the paper towel throwing it in the trash. The clerk wipes down the sink winking his eye at Brown through the mirror. Brown exits the restroom to catch his flight.

Over in Virginia Brown is driving his rental car to meet up with Alex and his crew. He texts while driving. *"Dude, I'm in route."*

Alex quickly responds, *"See you there."*

Fifteen minutes later at the restaurant Brown walks inside the sports bar, takes a look around before spotting Alex. The hostess, wearing blue jean shorts and a T-shirt, approaches Brown. "How many in your party, Sir?"

Brown points over in Alex's direction, "I'll be dining with them."

She smiles, "Oh, they're regulars here. Right this way." She turns to lead Brown to the table, but he could not resist looking at her nice ass in those shorts. "Here you are, Sir. Your waitress will be Angel today. She'll be right over to take your order."

Alex and Brown shake hands. "How's life treating you?"

Brown with a stern look, "I'm good. Let's get down to business. I have a plane to catch."

"It's like that? I thought you would stay for a while?" Alex asks.

"Nothing personal, I just have to get back."

Alex nods his head in agreement. "Okay, you're the boss." Alex tilts his head to the side before looking around the room. He places a medium sized jewelry case on the table. Brown observes as Alex opens the case. "I decided to include the latest iPhone," Alex says.

The phone just glimmers like a new car in the showroom. Brown reaches for the phone, and Alex quickly grabs it, removing it from the package. Brown just stares as Alex powers up the phone. Alex gives a signal to his partner to come and get the device. He takes the device to the ATM in the room. "Always make sure that the ATM you are inserting the device into doesn't have a camera. There's nothing in the device to stop the camera from recording."

Brown, on high alert, "I understand."

Alex leans back in his chair, "Just a matter of seconds before someone goes to the ATM." A young blonde woman walks over to the ATM. Brown just watches her and the phone. Once she inserts the card, Brown quickly turns his focus to the phone ... nothing happens.

"Dude, what's up?" Brown asks.

"Give it a second." Brown looks back at the young lady for a split second.

"Oh! Here it is! Hello Debra Fox, 1212 Van Cleef Road." Alex just smiles turning in Brown's direction.

Brown still not convinced. Alex shrugs his shoulders, "Is there something wrong?"

"Not at all, just waiting to see a little more," Brown responds.

A second person goes to the ATM and inserts his card. Brown glances over to the machine. *"Chris Tempel, 2314 Man Over Rd, VA, pin number 5518."* Alex chuckles, "This is too sweet! Would you agree?"

Brown is silent.

"Who do we have here? Oh … Samantha O'Reilly, American Express card holder. She has to have big bucks!" Alex says.

Finally, Brown cracks a smile followed by a big grin. "Okay, Alex, let's get down to business."

Alex signals for his partner, Tim, to go remove the device. "Typically, you want to use a restaurant or club. They usually don't have cameras on their ATMs, but it will work on any machine." Tim returns with the device. Alex places it back in the case. He powers down the phone, placing it back in the case sliding the case to Brown. "Now … where's the money? You have your device."

Brown slides Alex the small duffle bag. Alex unzips the bag. His eyes light up. "This isn't a hundred thousand?"

"No, it's not. It's fifty thousand."

"Where's the other half?"

"It's in the car."

Alex slightly irritated, "Why isn't it in this bag?"

"Just a couple of safety measures."

"Do I strike you as the type of guy who plays games? What I say, I do. I'm a man with integrity."

"Come on! Let's take a walk outside," Brown states.

"No, my friend, you and Mason can go outside. I'll stay right here with this package."

"Okay." Brown reaches for the medium sized jewelry bag. Alex stops him by placing his hand on top of the bag.

Brown looks up into Alex's face. Alex smiles. "It was a pleasure to do business with you, Mister."

"Brown!"

They shake hands, and Mason and Brown exit together. Alex quickly gets up leaving the restaurant.

Moments later Brown is pulling away in his rental. Mason walks around the corner jumping in a late model Cadillac SUV. He closes the door. Alex is sitting in the driver's seat. "You got it?"

"Yes Sir!" Mason responds

Tim turns around looking in the back seat, "Sam, Debra, Chris, y'all good?"

In unison, "YES, SIR!"

You should hear this dude mimic Alex. "I'm a man of integrity...."

Alex giggles, "Man please! Get out of here with that weak bullshit!" They all start laughing.

Back at Chicago Midway Airport Brown is getting off the plane. He has the swagger of a man who just won the lottery. He struts down the concourse headed outside to grab a taxi. He relaxes taking a deep breath as he admires the view of the city. *Nothing like being home.*

Octavius is still sitting around the apartment trying to crack that firewall. Brown enters the room with the biggest of grins on his face.

"What's happening, Dude?"

"What's got you all happy and shit?"

"Dude, you haven't changed clothes or anything. You've just been sitting here?"

"Why does that matter to you? All you care about is me getting through this firewall. You're starting to act like Fish Head, my old boss."

"Oct, Dude, it's of vital importance that we don't allow anyone to see what's going on! I apologize for the way I treated her, but the truth of the matter, she should not have been here ... period. Now if you want her around you knowing everything you do, that's fine. However, I can't have that. The less she knows, the better off she is."

Octavius lifts his head looking at Brown nodding that he agrees. "Man, Bro that still sucked the way you handled the situation."

"Trust and believe, she'll get over it."

Octavius with a half of smile, "You really think so?"

"Dude, she's feeling you."

"I don't know after the show she put on after you left. She was downright disrespectful to me, and a brother like Octavius don't play that disrespectful shit at all."

Brown chuckles, "Man, you ain't no G. Hell, you should have told her, Bitch, put some respect on my name!" They both start laughing.

Octavius laughing to tears came down, "Brown, you are a fool with it."

"Look, go get dressed. I want to show you how this new device works I just picked up. It's top flight."

Octavius quickly cuts off his laughter, "It's like that?"

"Dude, it's freaking awesome! I can't wait to show you how it works."

"What is it?"

"It's a micro magnetic card reader with a transponder."

Octavius giggles. "What? Dude, who have you been talking too? You sound all Geeky."

"Hurry up and get dressed."

Octavius gets up to freshen up walking to the bathroom. "Yeah, alright! That shit had better work because you hype." Brown sits at the computer gazing deeply into the screen. Moments later, Octavius comes out refreshed and ready to go.

"Dude, where did you get that gear from?"

Octavius grins. "Why? Do you like it?"

"I do. That's a good look for you. Gucci loafers with nice slacks. However, that tight ass white T-shirt not working unless you're going to put on a short sleeve shirt."

"Okay, give me a minute." Octavius walks in the back room and quickly returns wearing a solid black short sleeve shirt.

Brown shakes his head in agreement. "Nice."

Octavius tucks his shirt in revealing his Gucci belt with the double G's. "Now what was that about me not being a G? I'm a double G! GUCCI!"

They start to exit the condo. "Like I said you're not a G, more like drop the G and replace it with a C."

Octavius ponders for a split second. "Aw ... hell nah, Gucci! I see you got jokes now."

Brown bursts out in laughter. They get to the door. Octavius grabs his backpack.

"You're killing the fashion with that backpack. Leave it."

Octavius, with no hesitation, drops the backpack. Brown realizes that he has just about conformed Octavius to his standards.

At Club Nympho the line is around the corner. Octavius pulls up, as the valet rushes over to the car. Brown steps out of the car sliding one hundred dollars to the valet. Octavius steps out like he's being showcased on the Red Carpet Award show. He takes in the atmosphere, walking quickly to enter. The music is pounding when the doors open. It's packed inside, and the club is at capacity. Octavius and Brown follow the waitress to the VIP section. Octavius vibes to the music nodding his head. "Damn, Brown, even VIP is packed."

"Go ahead and order us a couple of drinks. I need to get over to the ATM."

Octavius smiles. "Don't even trip! I got cash."

"Why use your cash when you can use someone else's?"

Brown makes his way through the crowd, lights flash, and techno music pounding so hard you could feel the bass in your chest. A few people are ahead of Brown. He slides the clip from his inside pocket and inserts it into the ATM. He bends over like he's grabbing cash, turns and walks away. As he approaches the VIP section, he notices that Octavius has already invited a few women to the VIP. Brown makes his way around the VIP booth when one flirtatious Asian pinches his butt.

Brown, yelling over the music, "Dude, I see you got the party started without me?"

"Yes, Sir. I want you to meet Holly, Tasha, and China."

China, very attractive with one side of her head shaved, "Do you play for the Cubs too?"

Octavius winks his eye at Brown. "No, I don't play games," Brown responds.

China has the prettiest smile. "Oh, I see. You don't play games huh? Will you play with me?"

Brown sits looking at her breast sticking up out of her push up bra. "Yes, indeed, I would."

China slides a little closer to Brown. "Touch them." Brown scratches the back of his neck. China's lips move, and Brown reads her lips. "Touch them. I see you looking at them."

Brown looks at her. "Holly, is she for real?"

Holly just giggles. Brown realizes at that moment that China was high on pills.

Octavius, enjoying the moment, "Touch them, Bro."

Brown grabs his drink from the table and gulps it down. "Woo!" He turns and grabs China's breast with both hands.

China grabs both of his hands squeezing them into her breast. "You like?"

Tasha screams out, "THAT'S MY SONG!" Tasha and Holly head to the dance floor dragging Octavius along. China tries to convince Brown to dance with no luck. She joins Octavius and her girls on the dance floor. Brown pulls the device out powering it up. He sees several people in line for the ATM. Brown activates the phone to read the person's credit card at the ATM with no luck. Brown thinking that maybe he's too far away attempts it again with the next person in line. Again ... no luck. Brown quickly jumps up going to the restroom. He pulls out his cell phone to call Alex up in Virginia. He dials Alex's number it rings once. *"The number you are trying to reach is no longer in service. If you think you reached this number in error, please try again. Good bye!"* Instantly, Brown's heart starts to pound in his chest. "NO WAY!" He tries the number again ... same result. "NO FUCKING WAY!" He throws his cellphone on the floor smashing it.

The restroom attendant intervenes, "Sir, are you okay?" Brown looks in the mirror thinking about his worst fear. He's breathing heavy, and his eyes are turning bloodshot red. "Sir, is there something I can do? Or someone I should call?" the attendant asks.

"NO! Those sons of bitches going to pay!" Brown yells.

"Who, Sir? Are they in the club?" the attendant asks.

"NO!" He throws some water on his face, gets a paper towel and walks out the restroom back over to VIP. Brown sitting in disgust as China, Tasha, Holly and Octavius make their way back.

Octavius' adrenaline is high from dancing with three hot chicks. Octavius leans over to whisper into Brown's ear, "Dude, this China chick is feeling you."

Brown, unresponsive, stares out into the club.

Octavius yells, "DUDE! China is trying to get with you."

Brown mumbles, "You were right! They pulled one over on me!"

Octavius clueless, "Dude, what the fuck are you talking about?"

"The machine! Those guys got me for one hundred grand."

"One hundred large?"

Brown drops his head.

Octavius stunned, "Damn!" He falls back into his seat and notices that someone is blocking the light. When he looks up, Khloe and Cassie are standing right in front of him. Cassie is wearing a fitted mini dress that accents her beautiful body. Khloe is one of the hottest girls in the club tonight. Her makeup is flawless and so is her outfit.

Cassie snaps at Octavius looking at China, Holly, and Tasha. "Not even a week goes by, and you up in here with some other bitches?"

China instantly takes offense, "Who are you calling Bitch? Bitch!"

"I wasn't even talking to you! I'm talking to my man!"

Octavius chuckles, "Your man?"

Brown just looks on as the conversation intensifies. Khloe tucks her small purse under her arm. Cassie and Holly start to exchange words. Tasha tries to defend her friends getting in the argument.

China gets in Cassie's face, "Skank, you are not about that life. Stand down, Bitch!"

Out of nowhere Khloe smacks the hell out of China with her small purse. China falls over to the side. Cassie starts to kick China while she's trying to get up. Brown thinking that someone just turned off the lights, when four big security guards sweep all five ladies off their feet. All the women are kicking and screaming at one another. Brown quickly makes his way over to the ATM with Octavius on his heels. He removes his device from the ATM before disappearing out the club. The security escorted Cassie and Khloe out the front of the club and Tasha, Holly, and China out the back of the club. Khloe looks over at her friend, "Cassie, are you okay?"

Cassie's eyes are red from anger, "I can't believe this lame trying to play me?"

"Don't front, Girl. Just admit your feelings for him are deep."

Cassie's eyes tear up, "No ... that's not it." A tear falls from Cassie's eye. Khloe embraces her.

"It's okay, just admit to me that you got caught up in Octavius."

She gives Khloe a hard stare trying to regain her composer, "Bitch, it ain't even like that!"

Khloe laughs. "Yeah, okay! I get it! You never had a man to cater to you the way Octavius does."

Cassie sadly replies, "You're right. But, why you all up in my business you need to check yourself!"

Khloe confused. "What? This isn't about me. Don't get it confused."

Cassie forces herself to slightly laugh, "Yeah, this is! Your butt is lopsided because your dress is twisted up."

"Girl, thirsty as these guys are out here tonight, one cheek could be bigger than the other, they would not care!" She adjusts her dress. They both laugh as they're getting into the Uber cab.

Back at the condo Brown and Octavius sit in the room looking out over the city skyline. Brown recalls the entire transaction with Alex. Brown explains it and goes over each detail as if it was taking place. Octavius is hanging on to every word while visualizing the scenario. Octavius interrupts Brown, "So what you are saying is that you saw the device work?"

"Several times, I watched the people go over to the ATM insert their cards. In a matter of seconds their information appeared on the phone. I even watched him pay the tab with one of the stolen card numbers."

Octavius sits in deep thought rubbing his hands together. "Bro, let me see the phone." Brown tosses over the phone. Octavius activates the phone and goes to the setting. He's looking over all downloads and apps looking for information that could lead back to Alex. Brown is trying to contact Alex with no luck. Brown continues to call while anticipating his next move.

Octavius blurts out, "Ah Ha! Bro, these numbers were stored in the phone. This device is bogus, but it's a clever concept." Octavius continues to stroll around in the phone with no regard to how it made Brown feel. He glances over at Brown. Brown has a look of rage as he continues rocking from side to side. "Bro, you okay?"

Brown didn't say a word.

Octavius determined to find a link to Alex, searches Gallery in the phone. After another 20 minutes of scrabbling through the phone, Octavius finds credit card numbers with names attached.

Brown mumbles, "Those numbers are probably burnt."

"Yeah, maybe. What's interesting is that these numbers and names were put in this phone."

Brown thinks deeply about how it played out. "So, it's possible that he could have used people's information that he already knew. O'Reilly?" Brown says, cutting Octavius' words off.

"The good thing is that some of the people he used are probably legit."

"What the fuck was I thinking?" Brown asks out loud. Brown stares out at the city skyline, "Octavius, go home!"

"Bro, why? We can get these fools!"

Brown, in a stern voice yells, "GO HOME!"

Octavius a little shook up, "Alright, if you say so, but we are so close to breaking down that firewall."

Brown turns, looking at Octavius with death in his eyes, "Dude, leave!" He doesn't finish his sentence. Brown walks over to the window talking out loud to himself, *"What the fuck else can go wrong. Ivan's locked up. I just got taken for one hundred grand."* He takes a deep breath, *"What's next?"* Brown turns to walk out of the condo, and the computer starts chirping like a bird. He glances over at the computer, turns off the lights, double locks the door, and continues to his condo down the hall, shaking his head in disgust.

Octavius, back at his apartment, has started to search for those names in the phone on social media. His cell phone buzzes. He grabs it to look at the text. *"I apologize for the way I behaved at the club. Please forgive me."* Octavius smirks but continues to search the internet for information.

Khloe sits in Cassie's living room drinking some wine. Khloe admires Cassie's new décor. "Girl, your place is really coming together. Who helped you furnish the place?"

Cassie's eyes widen, "You know who. Why are you even asking?"

Khloe crosses her legs and leans back on the couch. "If he's doing all this and you haven't given him any, hmmm, you better hurry up before I give him some. Hell, I can use some new furniture."

Cassie starts laughing, "He only has eyes for me."

Khloe pats her butt, "Maybe until he gets a look at this ass."

Cassie bursts out in laughter, "Chick, you don't even have any ass."

"Yeah, I know, but you got too much! Besides I'm feeling Brown."

"Like you want to go down on Brown?" Cassie asks.

"Yeah, that too. Real talk, Girl, are they drug dealers?"

"Girl, Octavius' lame ass is no drug dealer," Cassie responds.

"Okay, so what's their deal? He's not repairing that many computers."

Cassie picks up her glass, takes a long sip, "They crack cards."

"Bitch, no they don't!"

Cassie nods yes as she sips on her drink. "Yes, they do."

"They must really be good at that shit? We have got to learn."

"Octavius has been showing me a little whenever we go shopping."

Khloe sits up on the end of the couch with the most serious look. "Cass, we have to get crack'in. This one guy I deal with from time to time has something going with credit cards. He's always saying that he can fix anyone's credit. I overheard him talking to a client one night."

"Bitch, did he fix your credit?"

"No! I don't have bad credit that needs to be fixed. Whore, let me finish. They were talking about some CPN numbers. He told that guy that he could have him in a brand new Porsche within a week."

"Okay, did he do it?"

"I don't know, but I did do a little research on CPN numbers."

Cassie refills her glass. "Okay, Girl, what is a CPN number? You got me all charged up now."

"CPN means Credit Privacy Number. It's supposed to replace your Social Security number. It's more like a second Social Security Number."

Cassie questions, with a serious demeanor, "Is it legal?"

"Bitch, Google it! This isn't Credit Class 101."

They both start laughing. Khloe lifts her glass up, "Pour me some more wine, please!"

"You know I'm going to look into that CPN stuff."

"Good, then you can tell me how it works. Meanwhile, you better give Octavius some of that biscuit."

"Girl, shut up!"

Just a few floors up, Octavius has completed his social media search on a couple of the credit card numbers that were stored in the phone. He sits back in his seat just staring at the monitor with the information. He tries to call Brown. The phone just rings without an answer. He tries to call again, still no answer. He text's, *"Yo, it's your boy. I got some information on those cats that you were trying to locate. Get at me when you get some time."*

Octavius looks at the time on his Chopard® watch and smirks before deciding to head to bed. The next morning, he grabs his cell phone off the nightstand hoping that Brown has texted back. He let out a sigh of disappointment. While checking for text messages, he notices that he has two voice mails from his old boss, Mr. Fisher. He starts to listen to the first message but hangs up just as the message was about to begin.

The next week Ivan is sitting in the room with Attorney Goldstein. Ivan, wearing a Department of Correction jumpsuit, is looking pretty rough. He hasn't shaved in days.

"So, Ivan, what have you decided? I know you've had time to think about it."

"Yeah, I have, but what are the odds I can beat this case?"

Ms. Goldstein flips open her briefcase removing Ivan's file. "Well, the government will argue intent. That means you were in the process of using all those numbers recovered in the card reader had you not got arrested. Now restitution will play a major part of this case. It's a program under which an offender is required, as a condition of their sentence, to repay money or donate service to the victims of their crime."

"Oh! So this case isn't looking good for me, huh?"

"Not in the least bit. My advice to you is to think long and hard about your decision. Ivan, don't be selfish either! Think about your family. Eight to twelve years is a long time. However, if you cooperate, your sentence will be cut drastically. I'm not insisting that you do so, but it's the only way not to get a significant amount of time."

"So you're talking about me snitching, huh?"

"Yeah, if that's what you want to call it."

The guard pounds on the door. "Counselor, times up!" The guard opens the door. "Ivan, it's time get up!"

Ivan stands looking at Ms. Goldstein with a blank stare. The guards start to escort him to the door. Ivan pauses, "I ain't a snitch! It is what it is!"

Ms. Goldstein nods in disapproval, "Just keeping it G, right?"

Ivan nods his head, "YEP!"

Ms. Goldstein slides her file back into her briefcase. "Guard, hold on for a second." The guard stops in his tracks. "Ivan, just so that I understand where you're coming from with this G thang, what exactly does that mean?"

"Just keeping it G is good. No one snitched on me, so why should I snitch? It's G." The guard raises his eyebrows out of respect for Ivan before walking him back to his cell.

The guard whispers to Ivan, "I must commend you for your courage, but this is not a game. The state's attorney will push for the maximum sentence." Ivan reaches his cell block looking back. The guard removes the cuffs and opens the cell door. Ivan never responds to his comment stepping into his cell. The guard closes the cell door. "I hope you feel where I'm coming from?"

Ivan just nods his head as the other inmates look at him. Ivan is about to breakdown when one of his cell mates interrupts. "Man, Bro, what that bitch made Officer Castle talking about?"

Ivan is slightly intimidated by Big Randy. Big Randy was one of the city's drug lords. Ivan hesitant, "He wasn't talking about shit."

Big Randy, mad at the system, could care less for anyone wearing a uniform. "Man, Lil Bro, don't trust any of them. You feel me?"

"Trust and believe I don't," Ivan replies.

A few days go by and Octavius hasn't heard from Brown. On his way out of the apartment building he doubles back to the front desk to talk with the receptionist. "Hey, Connie!"

"Hello, Octavius. What can I do for you, Sir?"

"I have a delivery coming today. Is it at all possible that someone could let them into my apartment?"

"Sure! What time are you expecting it to arrive?"

"This afternoon, before 3:00." Octavius pulls 20 dollars off his bankroll. "Thanks, Connie, lunch is on me."

Connie reaches for the cash, "Thanks, young man."

Octavius turns to walk out the building while tracking Uber on his phone. Cassie strolls up without him even noticing. Cassie, in a soft pleasant voice, "So you weren't going to return my calls or texts?"

Octavius looks away from his phone at Cassie. He is very surprised to see Cassie looking like a Diva, rocking some Christian Louboutin red bottom shoes and smelling great. Her presence forces Octavius to smile and wonder. "Yeah, I was going to get back to you. I've just been pretty busy with business. Look at you though! You out here stunting!"

Cassie blushes, "Not really."

"You're all *designered* out. What do you mean?"

"Thanks!"

The Uber car pulls up. "There's my ride."

"Octavius, where are you off to?"

Octavius' eyebrows raise, "Why?"

"I was hoping we could spend some time together."

"Okay, come go with me now."

"Are you sure? I don't want to impose on you or anything."

"Naw, just going to buy a car today."

Cassie intrigued, "Oh really." She makes her way over to the Uber car. Inside the Uber car Octavius and Cassie share views of their relationship. "Octavius, it's no secret how I feel about you."

Octavius, caught off guard, leans back away from Cassie, "Really, how do you feel? It's a secret to me."

Cassie smiles and laughs reaching over grabbing his hand. Octavius just enjoys the hand massage. "Now Cassie, what's really going on?"

Cassie's cell phone rings. She looks at the screen, and it's Khloe calling on Facetime. She answers, "Hey, Girl!"

"Hey, Cass!" Cassie turns the phone so that Khloe can see Octavius in the car. "Oh! I see you with Mr. O."

"Say hello, Octavius."

Octavius, very nonchalantly, "Hey, Khloe!"

"Dang, Mr. O, you don't have to be all dry!"

Cassie starts laughing, "Girl, stop tripping with my man."

"Oh really, your man?"

"Yes, my man."

"Whatever! Anyway, Girl, I'm going to dinner with Mr. T."

Octavius interrupts, "What's up with this Mr. O and Mr. T? You can't remember names or you trying to be secretive and what not?"

"No, Mr. O, I do remember names, maybe someone is around, and I don't want them to know who I'm talking too."

Octavius just nods his head towards the screen. Cassie turns the phone back to her. "Okay, we at the dealership."

"DEALERSHIP? What? Girl, are you about to get a new car?"

"I wish. Mr. O is about to get a new car."

Khloe frowns and nods her head yes, "Okay, I see you big time."

"Bye, Girl."

"Cassie ... wait."

"What, Girl?"

"Not you Octavius."

Cassie turns the phone in Octavius' direction, "What's up, Khloe?" Cassie steps out of the Uber car, and Octavius slides across the seat to get out on the same side.

"You see that fat ass in front of you. Smack it for me."

Octavius nods in disagreement as he steps out the car. Cassie starts laughing. "Girl, bye!"

Octavius opens the door of the BMW dealership. Cassie walks in first as Octavius looks down at her nice ass. The people in the dealership quickly run over to introduce themselves to Cassie. Octavius' phone rings. He quickly glances down at the screen. "Cass, I got to take this call. It's Brown."

"Okay, Sweetie. I'll just start looking around."

Octavius goes back outside to answer the call. "What's up, Bro?"

"Not much. I'm down here in Virginia."

"What? Why? Do you know who you are looking for?"

"No! I just went back to the couple of spots where we met. I figured that they would return sooner or later to the spot."

"Brown, that's crazy, Bro. I got the information on a couple of those people. The crazy part is that they have Facebook accounts."

Brown laughs. "I thought they would be a little smarter than that. Send that information to me."

"Bro, you need me to get on the next flight."

Brown chuckles. "For what? I need to handle this. Send that info."

"For sure. It's done. Say no more." Brown ends the call without a word.

Octavius takes a seat outside the dealership, scrolling through his phone attaching files to his message to forward to Brown. Cassie walks outside. "Octavius, I found a convertible that I think you might like."

"Is that right? Or is something that you like?"

"Whatever!" Cassie smirks and holds the door for Octavius to enter. When Octavius walks pass Cassie she slaps him on the butt. He laughs.

"What's up with that? You wouldn't like it if I did that to you in public?"

"How would you know if you never tried it?"

Octavius giggles. Cassie leads him over to a late model BMW convertible. The salesman walks over to introduce himself to Octavius extending his hand never taking his eyes off Cassie. "Hello, Octavius. I'm Bob."

Octavius, kind of annoyed, "Hey, Bob! Do you have any women salespeople here?"

Bob, a middle aged, white guy, responds "Yes, but why do you ask?"

"I just seem to have my way with women." Octavius slaps Cassie on the butt. She burst out laughing, stepping closer to Octavius.

Bob smirks. "Oh, I see. I'll get the first available saleslady to assist you." Bob turns to walk away.

Cassie starts laughing, "You're silly."

"I guess you do like it. You didn't say anything."

"No, I love it!" She kisses Octavius on the cheek.

At that very moment a young black woman walks over in the most seductive way catching Octavius' attention. "Hello, Octavius. I'm Sharon," extending her hand, "I'll be your salesperson today."

Octavius flirting, "If you're sharing, I'm buying."

Sharon blushes. "You're funny."

"No, I'm straight," Octavius responds.

Cassie, slightly jealous, "Are we going for a test drive or what?"

Sharon gives Cassie a hard look. "Yes, we can go for a test drive. Who's the buyer here?"

Cassie, with an attitude, "Why?"

Sharon says very politely, "Because I'm going to need that person's driver's license before we can test drive. Will that be a problem?"

"NO! That's not a problem." Octavius goes into his wallet pulling out his credentials. He hands them to Sharon.

"I'll be right back. I just need to make a copy and get a license plate for the car." Sharon turns to walk away.

Cassie, with a hint of anger in her voice, "Octavius, you had better not turn around and watch her."

Octavius giggles. "DANG! I never thought that I would see you act like this." He pulls her close to him. "Truth be told, she ain't got shit on you!"

Cassie smirks, "Yeah, I know. Now get up off me."

"DANG! That's cold." They both turn to walk toward the door for the test drive.

*   *   *

In Virginia, Brown is sitting in the restaurant where he met Ivan. He's sipping on a cold beer when a recognizable face appears in the corner of his eye. His cell phone buzzes showing a text from Octavius. *"These are the names and the faces of the people whose credit card numbers were in the phone."* Brown glances down at the screen and looks across the room to see Samantha O'Reilly sitting alone at the bar. Samantha is tall, thin with big boobs and a very pretty face. Brown chuckles to himself as he makes his way across the room. "Excuse me, is this seat taken?" Brown asks.

Samantha looks over her shoulder at this attractive man standing beside her. "Not yet, but I'm sure it will be if you sit down."

Brown sits down looking at Samantha through the mirror of the bar. "May I ask your name?"

"Sam!"

Brown thinking to himself, she may remember the name Brown. "I'm Tate. Nice to meet you."

"You as well, Tate, but I know your mother didn't give you the first name Tate?"

"No, she did not. However, I know your mother didn't just name you Sam? You're too pretty for such a short name."

Samantha smiles. "Okay, Mr. Smooth. Thanks for the compliment. Now what is it I could do for you?"

"I really just came over to ask about the signature dish to order in this establishment."

"It's a sports bar. WINGS!" Samantha states, while holding back her laughter.

"Speaking of wings, it was your wings that brought me over here," Tate says.

Samantha, kind of charmed, nodding her head, "No ... no ... no, Tate, I know you didn't try to hit me with the Angel line?"

"Well, if the truth is to be told and you heard it before, it has to have some validity."

Samantha smiles using her eyes. "Validity huh?" She gives like an inverted laugh trying not to just laugh in Tate's face.

"What?" Tate asks.

"Nothing. Where's your phone?" Samantha asks.

"Right here in my pocket." Brown removes the phone from his pocket.

"Unlock it!" Samantha says, reaching for the phone. Brown unlocks the phone, and Samantha quickly programs her number in the phone. "I have to get back to work. Call me later, tourist. We don't dress like that around here."

Brown looks down at his attire as Samantha walks away. "What?" She looks back with a big smile on her face walking out the door. Brown smiles back watching her hair and butt bounce out the door.

The bartender walks over. "Excuse me, Sir, are you picking up that tab?"

Brown starts laughing, "I guess I am. Here I'm thinking that I was baiting her in."

"Whatever! Let me get that bill for you." Brown leans back in his seat with a silly grin on his face.

Back at the dealership Octavius is filling out the loan application. Cassie and Octavius are sitting inside of Sharon's office. Sharon processes Octavius information. "Octavius, I see here on the application that you are a computer programmer."

"Yes."

"May I ask if you design websites?"

"Not normally, but I have done a few."

Cassie has her legs crossed and is getting a little annoyed by Sharon's questions. Sharon leans forward pulling her hair back behind her ear. "You missed a couple lines here, lines 17 and 20." She turns the clipboard pointing to the lines. Octavius scoots to the edge of his seat to fill them in. Sharon and Octavius' eyes lock. "I'm having problems with my graphic designer. Do you think it's possible to get some assistance from you?"

Cassie's leg starts swinging back and forth thinking to herself, *No, Bitch! He's not doing anything for you.*

"I don't have a problem with that."

Sharon looks right over Octavius into Cassie's face. Cassie just smirks.

Cassie and Octavius are on a test drive when Cassie's cell phone rings. "Hello!"

"Hey, Girl! What's all that noise in the background?" Khloe asks.

"Girl, Octavius is test driving a convertible BMW, and the top is down."

"Nice. Well, Girl, I'm going to hook up with the old man tonight."

"Who?"

"Mr. Credit Repair."

"Oh yeah! I'm handling my end. You handle yours. I'll have him eating out of my hand."

Cassie giggles. "Is that all you want him to eat?"

"That's a must with the old man."

Cassie giggles. Sharon is in the back sit. "Turn left up at the corner."

"Who was that?" Khloe asks.

Cassie frowns. "The salesperson."

"Okay, Girl. I'll let you know how it goes."

"Okay!"

*   *   *

Brown is sitting in his hotel room plotting his next move. He is thinking about texting Samantha. He smirks at the thought of her innocence, very pretty and simple. His cell phone chirps! He looks down, and it's a text from Samantha. He laughs. *HEY, TATE! WHAT ARE YOU DOING LATER? WANT TO HANG OUT?*

Brown suspicious, *YES, I WOULD LIKE THAT. WHERE WOULD YOU LIKE TO MEET AND WHAT TIME?*

YOU PICK THE TIME AND PLACE. TOURIST!

LOL...OKAY! LET'S MEET AT THE OCEANFRONT HILTON AROUND 7:00.

WOW! OKAY! WHAT LINE OF WORK DID YOU SAY THAT YOU WERE IN?

I DIDN'T, BUT WE CAN DISCUSS ANYTHING YOU LIKE OVER DINNER. SEE YOU AT SEVEN.

SEE YOU THEN, TATE.

Brown opens up his computer and starts looking for the others that were involved in taking his hundred grand.

* * *

Back at the BMW dealership Octavius has decided to buy a certified BMW convertible black on black. Sharon is getting the last minute details together while the car is being cleaned. Cassie is getting restless. "I never knew that buying a car takes all day. We've been here for over five hours."

Sharon, with a devious smirk, "So are you saying that you've never bought a new car?"

Cassie's neck snaps back with her head tilted thinking to herself, *I know this bitch just didn't try to front on me.* Cassie gives Sharon the stare down.

Octavius glances over at Cassie's expression, grabbing her hand, "It's not going to be much longer, Sweetie. I know you're ready to go." The porter walks in the office to bring the keys to the car.

"Thanks, Tim," Sharon says.

Cassie pulls her hair back behind her ear and lets out a deep breath. Octavius places his hand on her thigh to calm her. She begins rocking. Sharon, observing how attentive Octavius is with Cassie, is slightly jealous, "*Spoiled!*"

"Are we done here?" Octavius asks.

"Just waiting on the insurance company to send over proof that you're covered."

"Cass, take the keys and go ahead and sit in the car."

Cassie thinking to herself, "*And leave you here with this thirsty bitch*?" "No, Babe, I'm okay right here."

Moments later the insurance card shows up. "It was my pleasure doing business with you. Here's my card with my work and personal numbers. Please give me a call if you have any questions about anything." Sharon shakes Octavius' hand.

"Thank you for your service," Octavius says.

"Maybe I'll be thanking you later for service, if you're still going to take a look at my website?"

"That's no problem. Give me a call, and we'll set something up."

Cassie turns to walk out, and Octavius is right on her heels. Once in the car Cassie hasn't said a word. Octavius, enjoying the moment, drives over to Brown's condo. He pulls up in front. "I'll be right back. I need to run up to Brown's apartment really quick to check something."

"Okay! Hurry back! I'm starving!" Cassie responds.

Octavius walks quickly into the building showing the key pass. He steps off the elevator in high gear to the apartment. He inserts his key pass. It beeps. He tries to turn the door handle. Confused he tries it again. At that moment he realizes that the code has been changed. He tries to call Brown. "Come on, Bro, pick up." No answer. Octavius, wanting to get inside to check the computer, walks off. He turns and walks back down to the lobby. He jumps back inside the car.

"That was quick," Cassie says.

"Yeah, I know. I told you it would be quick. You want to do some shopping?"

Cassie's eyes light up. "Only if you are going to show me how you do it? I would like to get nice things for you. I just can't afford to get the things I think you would like."

Octavius smirks. "Let me think about it." He puts the car in drive and pulls away quickly. "Now, if I agree to show you how it's done, what's in it for me?"

Cassie turns, looking directly at Octavius, "What is it you want?"

"I don't know. What are you willing to give?" Octavius asks.

"All of me *plus*!"

"Plus what?" Octavius asks.

"You name it. I'll game it."

Octavius is starting to get aroused. "Okay, it's a deal." Thinking to himself, "*You don't have to do anything. Your company is enough.*" Cassie leans over and kisses Octavius on the ear while grabbing his cock.

At the Outlet Mall Cassie is walking with plenty of bags, Macy's, Gucci, and others. Cassie's smile is bright. Octavius exhausted, "Okay! I've shown you how it's done. Did you catch on? It's really nothing to it. It's really just shopping."

"I got the shopping part down. I need to know how to load a card."

"I got you, all in due time. It's getting late. Why don't we just grab a pizza and take it back to my place?" Cassie asks.

"That works for me."

At the Oceanfront restaurant Tate (Brown) is waiting for Samantha. It's a very beautiful evening with a nice cool breeze. The patio setting is like a tropical island. He scrolls through his contacts on his phone. The waiter comes over to the table speaking with a foreign accent, "Sir, will you be dining alone?"

"No, she's on her way."

"Can I start you off with something to drink?"

"Yes, bring me a double shot of Johnnie Walker Blue label."

"Yes, Sir." The waiter turns to walk away bumping into Samantha standing behind him. "I'm so sorry, Madam."

"No, it was my fault. You didn't know I was standing behind you."

Tate (Brown) admires Samantha's attire. She is wearing an orange fitted dress with white lace across the back and white Stilettos. The waiter pulls her seat out. "Can I get you something to drink, Madam?"

"I'll have whatever he's drinking," Samantha says.

"Why no, Madam, I don't think you want something that potent."

Tate (Brown) chuckles for a moment, "If that's what the young lady wants."

The waiter steps to the side of Samantha and pulls out his writing pad, "Are you sure that Johnnie Walker Blue label is what you want?"

Samantha looks at the waiter and nods, "Yes, I'm sure."

"Okay, Madam, one double Johnnie coming right up." The waiter turns walking away quickly.

Samantha, flirting with Tate, "You don't look like a tourist now."

Tate grins, "Is that right? You look nothing like I thought you would. I had you figured for the jeans and t-shirt type of girl."

"Is that right? Now what made you think that?"

"You seem kind but a little rough around the edges." Samantha's smile is so bright you can't help but to smile when she smiles.

The waiter returns with their drinks. "Here you go, good people. Have you decided what's for dinner?"

"Sam, order whatever you like," Tate says.

Samantha, while glancing at the menu, "May I please have the New York strip steak, medium rare, with a house salad?"

"Yes, Madam, and for you, Sir?"

"The same, but the New York strip steak, well done please."

"Will either of you have any type of potatoes?"

"No, thank you." Samantha replies.

"Naw!" Tate responds.

"Okay, your order and hot bread will be out soon." He turns walking off.

"What a beautiful night," Samantha says.

"Yes, and it's getting better the more I look at you," Tate says.

Samantha blushes. "Where do you come up with these pickup lines?"

"I'm speaking the truth. They're not pick up lines. You're already here," Tate says.

"That's true," Samantha replies.

Tate grabs his drink, holding it in the air, "Bottoms up!" Samantha joins Tate as they both take down their drinks.

"WOO!!" Samantha says.

Tate just frowns for a second, "Now that's good liquor."

*   *   *

Back at Cassie's apartment they have eaten the pizza and started drinking alcohol. Octavius sits back in the living room listening to some R&B music. Cassie's in the other bedroom. Octavius' phone buzzes. *"Hey, Octavius! This is Sharon. I was wondering how the car is working out for you?"*

"The car drives like a dream. I can't be more satisfied. Thank you!"

"You're welcome. However, you still need to take me for a ride!"

Octavius' devious mind, *"Are you talking about the car or you?"*

"Which ever you prefer! LOL!"

Octavius sits there grinning, preparing to text again when Cassie walks in the room. "Who in the hell got you grinning?" Cassie asks.

"Nobody, I was just thinking about something that happened the other day. It was pretty funny."

"Okay let me hear it!" Cassie says.

"No, it was one of those you had to be there to really get it."

"Oh, it was that chick Sharon from the BMW dealer."

Octavius sits up straight, slightly nervous like he just got caught cheating, "Naw!"

"It's okay though." Cassie walks over, dims the lights, then stands in front of Octavius. Octavius looks up to Cassie from the couch. He reaches out to Cassie. She sits beside him. "It's okay, only because I got you here with me." She kisses Octavius very passionately. Octavius grabs her breast aggressively. Cassie in a very soft voice, "It's yours. I'm not going to take it back. Easy!" She starts to remove her shirt and bra while Octavius can only anticipate. Her shirt hits the floor followed by her bra. Octavius leans forward, rubbing his hand across her flat stomach up to her firm breast before sucking and licking on her nipples. He kisses his way back down to her waist removing her jeans. She stands over him in her thong as he rubs over her entire body. She pulls her hair back into a ponytail then bends over and removes Octavius' shirt. Cassie was shocked to see that Octavius was chiseled for such a thin guy. Cassie walks over to turn the lights off just so Octavius could get a good look at her ass. He became more aroused watching her sexy walk. He removes his pants and underwear before she could return to him. The only light in the room was the moonlight. She greets Octavius with another deep passionate kiss getting him even more aroused. He squeezes her ass in the palms of his hands. She leads him to her bedroom.

*   *   *

After dinner, Tate convinces Samantha to come up to his room. Samantha, standing out on the balcony enjoying the view as the wind blows softly, removes her shoes while staring out into the dark ocean. She closes her eyes for a moment listening to the waves hit the shore. Tate startles Samantha walking up behind her placing his hands on her waist. Samantha jumps slightly turning around to face Tate. "Are you okay, Sam?"

"Yes! You just caught me by surprise." She looks deep into Tate's eyes. "What's really going on here? You seem so kind, but I see sadness in your eyes."

"I'm fine, just like you are to me one fine woman."

Samantha laughs, "There you go with those pickup lines. I'm really feeling you, and I haven't been treated like a real woman in such a long time."

"That's only because you haven't been with a real man."

Samantha pulls Tate close hugging him tight. Her eyes start to tear up. "Thanks for everything, Tate, but I have to go."

She tries to pull away. Tate pulls her close and whispers in her ear, "Let me make you feel like a woman." He begins kissing her on the neck. She tilts her head back exposing her neck. She grabs the back of his head kissing him passionately. She turns away looking out to the ocean. Tate stands behind her kissing the back of her neck. She pulls her hair to the side Tate kisses her back while squeezing her voluptuous breasts. She slides the dress off her shoulders spins around with her breasts exposed.

Tate looks deep into Samantha's eyes before taking her breast into his mouth.

In a low intoxicating voice, "Make me feel like a woman if only for one night." Her dress falls down, and she steps out of it. She stands on the balcony in her thong. Tate slides her thong to the side placing his finger into her wetness. Samantha moans, "Yesss!!!"

Tate aroused, loses focus of his reason for even being in Virginia. He gets caught up in the moment. "You want it out here?"

Samantha, breathing heavily, "Yes, Baby! Right here and right now!" The breeze blows across Samantha's body. She turns out to the ocean arching her back on the rails. Tate begins to unfasten his clothes. Samantha spins around to watch Tate undress while playing with her breast. Once his manhood is exposed she drops down taking him deep in her throat. Tate's knees buckle from this intense feeling. He braces himself on the rails while Samantha has her way with him. She looks up at him while stroking his penis back and forth. He reaches down for her hand spinning her around on the balcony rail. She arches her back closing her eyes in anticipation of Tate's penetration. Tate slides on a condom quickly then positions himself to gently enter Samantha. "OOH YESS!!! Take me I'm yours."

*   *   *

Back in Chicago Khloe begins to implement her plan. She's riding inside Tyrone's Bentley Flying Spur. Tyrone is driving when his cell phone rings. He quickly answers using the car's Bluetooth system. "Hello!"

"How's it going, Ty?"

"I'm good. What about yourself?"

"I'm well. I was calling to confirm if you had completed the credit profile numbers?"

"Everything is just about ready to go. One more question, are you going to need a D&B number, or are you just doing this personally as a SCN?"

"What's SCN?"

"SCN is a Secondary Credit Number, and CPN should be connected to corporate structure."

"Right, I forget sometimes."

Khloe sits there like a sponge listening and flipping through her cell phone. Tyrone is unknowingly being recorded by Khloe. Tyrone, trying to impress Khloe, "This package set you back about twenty-five grand."

"That's fine, Ty. I have something already lined up for a hundred grand."

"This line will be an easy two hundred fifty thousand."

"That's sweet."

"Alright, Cory, I got my little friend with me."

"Okay. Later."

Tyrone looks over at Khloe, "You know what I like most about you?"

Khloe looks at Tyrone thinking to herself, *The way I suck that old limp dick of yours?* No, I don't Tyrone. What is it you like best about me?

Tyrone pulls into a five-star hotel. "The fact that when I'm taking care of business you never interrupt, and the way you perform on me orally." Tyrone starts laughing. Khloe is slightly annoyed by that statement.

"Why are we here? Don't you have to get home to your wife?"

"No, she's gone out of town to my daughter's school. She won't be back for a week. So that means you have me for a week."

Khloe fakes her excitement, "That's great." The valet opens the car door for her. Khloe thinks to herself, "*a week with this clown is going to be bad. What the hell am I going to do with a 60-year-old man for a week?*"

*   *   *

The next day, Octavius gets a text from his old boss, Mr. Fisher. *HEY THERE, OCTAVIUS! MY DAD WILL BE IN TOWN TOMORROW. PLEASE STOP BY THE STORE AROUND NOON.* Octavius nods his head in approval. He looks down closer to the screen realizing the text was from the day before. He glances at the time. It's ten o'clock. He quickly gets dressed putting on the best clothes that money can buy. He dashes out the door and stops at the front desk. "Thanks for allowing the furniture company to deliver my bedroom set."

"It wasn't a problem, Mr. Smith," the female clerk says. Octavius pulls out a roll of cash. He removes a fifty-dollar bill giving it to the clerk.

"No, Sir, young man, that's too much!" The clerk insists that he take it back. Octavius smiles and walks away as if he didn't even hear a word. The clerk shakes her head in disagreement, *"What has the boy gotten himself into?"*

Octavius pulls up in front of his old job, and just like clockwork Fishhead is looking out the window. Octavius jumps out wearing Gucci shades, clothes, and shoes. Mr. Fisher quickly runs to the door to meet him. "That's a kick ass ride you got there."

Octavius removes his sunglasses. "Where's your dad?"

"He's in the back. Octavius, do me a favor?"

Octavius frowns and looks at Mr. Fisher, "What might that be Fishhead?"

"Tell my dad you're coming back, and don't call me that in front of him."

"What? After the way you treated me. You got to be kidding. I could think of a few worse names to call you."

Mr. Stanley Fisher Sr. emerges from the back office dressed in an Armani suit. A big smile appears on his face when he sees Octavius. He immediately walks over, extending his hand, "How's it going, young man?"

Octavius exchanges the sentiment, "Good, and you Sir?"

"I'm well, Octavius, but this store is another situation. This is what brought me to town. I was hoping that you and I could agree on some type of arrangement."

"What arrangement would that be, Sir?"

I was thinking that you and Junior could co-manage this store. Since you left our sales have declined."

"Wow! I was thinking that you were going to offer me more money, but never a management position. Thanks, Sir."

"So is that a yes? I'll double your salary."

"Wow! I'm very grateful, Sir, but I'm going to have to decline. It's nothing personal with you. I just can't see myself working with Junior anymore."

"Wow! Is Junior that bad?"

"I'm afraid worse."

"Hey, he takes after his mother." They both laugh.

Junior is pissed that Octavius declined the position. He storms off mumbling, *"Asshole … trying to front me off in my dad's presence! Yeah, okay!"*

"What was that Junior?"

"Nothing, Dad."

"You're fired!" Stanley Sr. says jokingly.

"What?" Stanley Junior asks.

"I'm joking. Get back to work. This store is outdated. Get some new technology around here. Well, Octavius, it's been a blast seeing you. I only wish that I could get you to take the job. I'll be here until tomorrow evening then I'm headed to New York. Give me a call between now and then one way or the other?"

They're about to embrace one another when Stanley Sr. sees a news flash from New York. "Junior, turn up the volume will you?" Stanley Jr. quickly grabs the remote. Everyone's attention shifts to the television monitor.

"Hi! I'm Chip Razor, reporting live from the studio. Never have I seen anything like this since the crash of the stock market. Attorney Henry Taylor, a known mob lawyer, allegedly jumped from the 30th floor of this office building. Inside sources say that he jumped after losing millions of dollars from the Grasso family empire. All this was caught on tape with a smartphone from ground level. Caution this may be a little too graphic for our viewers. (Henry Taylor's body is airborne then smacks the pavement.) Wow! For more details, log on to WERK.com, or tune in later to our evening news. Thanks, I'm Chip Razor and have a great afternoon."

Junior turns down the television. "Well ... that was hard to watch. People seem to be unfazed by death nowadays," Stanley Sr. says. Octavius stands there speechless wondering what would make a person jump out a window to his death. Stanley Sr. nods in disapproval, "Like I was saying. Give me a call, Octavius, if you change your mind." They shake hands, and Octavius walks out the store. Stanley Jr. just stares out the window in anger.

Octavius quickly pulls away. His cell phone begins ringing while he's driving. He answers the phone on his Bluetooth. "Hello!"

"Hey, Dude!" Brown says.

Octavius, with excitement in his voice, "What's up, Bro? When you coming back?"

"Tonight. I'm going to need you to pick me up."

"Okay! What I look like Uber to you?" Octavius asks.

"No, it's more like I need a Lyft." They both laugh.

"Okay, I got you. Don't even sweat it. Text me the time and the flight, I got you."

"Okay, Dude, I'll see you then," Brown says.

Octavius, feeling like a million bucks, just got offered his job back, at double the pay. His new best friend was on his way back to town, and Cassie has started to express real feelings for him.

*　　*　　*

Over in New York, the infamous Grasso family has gotten together at one of their signature restaurants. They own and operate fine dining, Italian style restaurants across the country, Buccus's. Sonny Grasso is the head of the family, and his nephew, Joey, is second in command. Sonny, a well-dressed, older man in his late 50's, is still seen as one of the mafia's most dangerous men. At the table eight of his henchmen sit waiting for orders. Joey, in his early 30's, medium build, makes the moves Sonny calls out.

Sonny, carving his steak, looks across the table to Joey. "Explain to me what happened at the Henry Taylor Law office today?"

Joey talks with a lot of hand gestures, "Okay, I took a couple of the guys over to the office. This damn secretary didn't want to let us go back to see Henry. I had to get a little loud."

Sonny nods while chewing his steak, "Okay...."

Joey hunches his shoulders. "Then we had to force our way back to the office. The secretary had already called back to announce our presence. She started yelling that we couldn't go back. By the time we got to the office, the office was empty, and the window was wide open."

Sonny grabs his napkin, wipes his mouth. "So what you're telling me is that Henry had already jumped before you made it back? Tell me now if you dropped Henry out that window or pushed him out?"

Joey stands firm, "No, Sonny. You gave a direct order to bring him back."

Sonny sits up straight, "Take Danny Boy and Joe Jr. and bring me the secretary alive. Do you understand me? ALIVE! I need to find out what happened to 22 million dollars ASAP before the other families realize it's gone." Sonny leans back in his seat as they leave out, "Sweet Mother Mary."

After a couple hours, Joey and the guys return with the secretary. Sonny and the guys are in the back room playing cards and smoking cigars. Joey leans down to whisper in Sonny's ear. "Boss, we have the girl in the next room."

Sonny jumps up from the table, "Excuse me, gentleman, I have some business to handle really quickly."

Joey and Sonny walk into the next room. Danny Boy is standing next to Beth Stallone. Beth is crying and shaking while Danny Boy stands behind holding her by the shirt. "DANNY BOY! That's not how you treat a lady. Release her shirt."

Sonny walks up to Beth bends over in her face and smacks the crap out of Beth. Beth falls back in her chair screaming, "PLEASE DON'T KILL ME."

Sonny, in a very scary tone, "That's all up to you. I'm only going to ask once. What the fuck happened to my money? Think about it before you speak. If I don't like your answer, you are not going to like my next move."

Beth just tells all as Sonny sits and listen. Sonny slightly confused, "So you telling me someone has stolen my money?"

Beth speaks softly through her tears, "Yes, Henry had been working extremely hard to recover your money."

Sonny rubs his palms together thinking to himself then blurts, "Then why would he kill himself?"

"I don't know. All I know is when these guys walked in his office I heard Henry screaming. Then I ran to his office, and these guys were laughing looking out the window," Beth responds.

Sonny looks around the room at Danny Boy, Joey, and Joe Jr. Sonny stands up walking towards Danny Boy and Beth. He extends his hand for her to get up. She grabs his hand slowly getting out of the chair. "I apologize for the way you've been treated here." Sonny places his hand on her back and kisses her on the cheek where he slapped.

"It's okay. I understand," Beth replies, closing her eyes as tears stream down feeling like she was about to die.

Sonny removes his hands, "Hey Beth! Open your eyes. I want you to forget about tonight, everything going to be just fine." He goes inside of Beth's purse taking her identification. "Just remember, we know where you stay and won't have a problem finding the rest of your family. Don't tell the cops anything. Do you understand me?"

Beth's face is bruised, and she's an emotional wreck. She is trying to gather her thoughts as Sonny stares in her eyes, "Okay, Mr. Grasso," Beth replies.

"Joey, give Ms. Beth some cash and send her home." Joey gives Sonny an odd look to say as if he meant kill her? "A couple grand, she knows to keep her mouth closed," Sonny says. He lights his cigar and walks away returning back to the card game.

* * *

That evening at O'Hare airport, Octavius is sitting waiting on Brown to come out. He spots Brown walking out and starts tapping on the horn slightly. Brown spots him and immediately walks over. Brown, with the biggest smile, "Hey! What's happening, Dude? Nice ride."

Octavius sits back all nonchalantly then gives off the biggest grin ever, "So you like the ride?"

Brown steps inside after putting his luggage in the trunk. "It's fair for a square like you."

Octavius frowns, "And what is that supposed to mean?"

"It means just what I said. It's fair for a square person like you. Myself, I'm a Mercedes man."

Octavius pulls off slowly navigating through airport traffic. "I don't know what you're thinking. Everybody is looking at my Black Man Working."

Brown laughs. "Yes, they are looking, but only because it's kind of cool out tonight and you got the top down with the heat on."

"Whatever! You're something like a hater!" Octavius says letting the top up.

Brown laughs. "No, Bro, this car is the shit!"

After about twenty minutes of driving Brown turns the radio down. Brown, with the sincerest look, "Dude, I want to apologize about the way I treated Cassie at the condo. If you say that's your lady, then I have to accept her for that."

"Thanks, Bro! However, you did set the rules about the condo. I shouldn't have brought her there. That's my bad."

"It's cool," Brown replies while looking out the window at the skyline.

"Hold up, B. What's going on? You were out of town with a woman?"

Brown's facial expression tells it all, "No, but I did meet someone who I found interesting."

"That's all good. Bro, that girl, Khloe, is looking really good these days. I know she wants some of that white chocolate."

Brown cracks up laughing. "Dude, where in the hell did you get this line? White Chocolate?"

"No, Dude, I'm good. She's just a gold digger."

"Bro, don't say that again. People don't say gold digger anymore."

Octavius pulls inside the underground parking lot at Brown's condo. "Okay! What do they say now, Mr. Know It All?"

"They say, she's thirsty!"

"Whatever, Dude! Thirsty or gold digger is all the same," Brown says.

They remove the suitcases from the trunk and head on up to the condo. Once inside they sit in the living room. Octavius gets up, walks over to the fridge and grabs a couple of cold beers. He opens up the bottle and takes a big gulp. "Ahh! That's nice and cold."

Brown leans forward on the couch in deep thought twisting his cap off the bottle. He takes a sip. "Dude, I haven't been in this situation in a long time. My guy, Ivan, locked up, VA just took me for a hundred grand, and on top of that, I'm down to my last thousand credit card numbers. When I was out of town, one of my clients wanted to buy one hundred numbers. I told him that I was out. He couldn't even believe it."

Octavius takes another sip of his beer, "Bro, we straight. Mr. Fisher offered me back my old job at double the salary."

"That's good for you, Dude. My monthly expenses are ten grand. I don't know what he's paying you, but it's not enough."

"I can get numbers from the store," Octavius suggests.

"No, that would be easy to track," Brown replies. He sits there in deep thought sipping on his beer.

*   *   *

Over at Cassie's place, she and Khloe are sitting around trying on designer outfits they just purchased. Cassie has the music on and uses her hallway as if it is a runway. Khloe walks out then Cassie, observing one another. Khloe sits there cheering for Cassie while she models a black and yellow two-piece suit. Cassie spins around in front of Khloe. Khloe smacks her on the ass. Cassie caught off guard, "Hey! What the hell was that for?"

Khloe starts laughing, "Girl, that ass is phat! You got like one of those stripper booties."

Cassie walks over, picks up her glass of wine and takes a deep breath. "What you don't have in ass you make up for with looks."

"Don't get me wrong, Bitch! I know I'm fine. However, it would be nice just to have a little more booty."

"If you want more booty, you know what you have to do?"

"No, what do I have to do?" Khloe asks.

Cassie starts dancing and singing. "You have to let him…. hit it from the back … hit it from the back … let him bang."

Khloe jumps up and starts dancing and laughing. "Girl, you crazy! I'm telling you now as soon as I get my hands on some money I'm getting a butt job."

"Whatever! You're fine just the way you are."

"Coming from the girl with the little waist and big ass," Khloe says.

"Okay, Girl! If you must have more ass, then we're going to need more cash."

Khloe shakes her head. "You are a mess, Cass." Cassie grabs her glass and they toast. "To more money!" Khloe says.

"To money it is," Cassie replies. Cassie finishes up her glass of wine. "Khloe, have you seen my cell phone?"

Khloe shakes her head, "Girl, don't drink anything else. It's sitting right there on the table behind you."

Cassie grabs the phone and takes a selfie. "Damn, I look a mess."

Khloe starts laughing. "There's nothing wrong with you."

"I know. I just wanted to hear you say it," Cassie replies.

"I can't stand you at times!" Khloe starts laughing.

"I'm about to send this picture to my man." Cassie sends the photo to Octavius.

Octavius still at Brown's condo, smiles looking at the picture. He replies to her text. *WHAT'S GOOD? I'M WITH BROWN.*

I KNOW. THAT'S THE ONLY TIMER YOU'RE NOT WITH ME. LOL!

I SEE YOU GOT JOKES. HA HA! LET ME FINISH UP OVER HERE WITH BROWN. IF IT'S NOT TOO LATE, I'LL COME UP TO YOUR PLACE.

I DON'T CARE WHAT TIME IT IS; I'LL MAKE YOU CUM!!!

YEAH, ALRIGHT!

Khloe looking at Cassie with a big grin on her face, "Bitch, why you looking all goofy?"

"Bitch, you know why. I'm going to ride that big goofy tonight."

Khloe shakes her head, "You know that you're really extra, right?"

"Yeah, whatever!"

The next morning Octavius didn't make it home. He slept on the couch. He sits up on the couch rubbing his eyes with a slight headache from drinking. He grabs his cell phone looking and checking his emails and text messages. Brown emerges from the shower. He walks into the living room with a robe on drying his hair. "Good morning, Dude."

"Good morning, Bro. Do you have an extra toothbrush?"

"Yeah, I have a spare travel bag that I keep just in case someone spends the night."

Octavius frowns, "A whore bag? You know women are going to find that offensive."

Brown wipes his face. "So you think? Only a whore will get mad. Real women will appreciate the fact I thought to do it, and the next time you spend the night bring your own bag, HOE!" They both start laughing.

"That's a $5,000-dollar sofa you're sleeping on."

Octavius rubs the leather. "This is the most expensive thing I've slept in or on."

"Naw, I think that would be Cassie." Brown starts laughing.

"Oh! I see you on a roll this morning. You coming for me like that?" Brown continues laughing.

"Bro, all jokes aside. Why did you lock me out the other condo? I went to check on the status of our project and couldn't get in. What's up with that, Bro?"

Brown turns and walks to the refrigerator and grabs a bottle of water. "Dude, everything was going great, then out of nowhere shit got bad and fast. I got frustrated and shut down. I just needed to get away." He sips on the water.

Octavius nods in agreement, "Bro, I can understand that." Octavius walks into the bathroom.

Moments later Octavius returns from the bathroom, and Brown is fully dressed in all black. "Damn, Bro, you going to a funeral or robbery? I do like those Gucci shoes and belt."

"Thanks. Let's go to the other condo so we can get back to work. We have to get some credit card numbers."

They exit the condo headed for the condo around the corner on the same floor. Brown sticks the keycard in the door to disable the alarm and opens the door. Brown enters with Octavius on his heels. Brown pauses, "What's that chirping sound?"

Octavius doesn't say a word. He quickly walks to the other room where the computers are set up. The chirping is coming from the computer. The bird on the screen was flying back-and-forth with a banner that reads, *"$21,000,000!"* Octavius shouts out, "YES!"

Brown quickly enters the room to see the bird flying across the screen. "What does that mean?"

Octavius smiles frantically, "It means we're in the money. Bro, 21 million dollars came out that one account. YESSS!!!"

All kinds of thoughts run through Brown's mind at once. How he was planning to kill someone for a hundred grand and now he has millions. He quickly comes back to his senses. "How long has it been here?"

Octavius sits quickly at the computers typing, "It's been here a week."

"Last week when I was locking up the condo, I heard a loud chirping sound but didn't think about it twice. How long does it take before someone could track the money?"

Octavius working very quickly to destroy the virus path, "It's done. How long would it take to track the money depends on how good the hacker or engineer is at tracking."

"How long would it take you?" Brown asks.

"It would depend on the amount of information that's available for the account."

*   *   *

Over in New York, Sonny is sitting in his beautiful home talking with Joey. They're talking at the table. Sonny's grandson, Tommy, sits across the room working on his computer. Joey always teases Tommy about not wanting any parts of the organization. Tommy just graduated from high school. "Tom, what are you doing over there? Looking at porn?" Joey says jokingly. "Whenever I see you, your head is buried inside that computer like a piece of ass." Joey laughs.

"Joey, leave Tommy alone. That's our future lawyer," Sonny says.

"I don't pay any attention to Joey. He knows nothing about what I do," Tommy says.

"What is it you do again?"

"I'm about to take the computer engineer test. I'm also a certified computer programmer."

Sonny's face lights up. "Hey, Tommy, what do you know about tracking?"

Tommy looks over at Sonny, "You need to know where the package is coming from and what company is shipping it."

Sonny frowns, "No, tracking on the computer."

"I don't understand. What it is you are asking me?" Tommy says.

Joey starts laughing. "Uncle, leave it to me. I'll get it done."

Sonny looks at Joey sternly, "You know sometimes Joey, you and your guys laugh at the wrong times. This is one of those times. Don't say another word or you'll regret it."

Tommy looks over at Joey. Joey grinds his teeth together and drops his head. Tommy smirks. "Now, Sonny, are you talking about hacking?"

"I want to track some money that has been stolen from one of the family accounts. Is that possible?" Sonny asks.

"Sure, if you have the account number, I could try. Let me grab my other computer." Tommy quickly walks away.

Joey feeling upset, "He doesn't dress like us or talk like us. Sonny, he's not one of us."

Sonny rises up out of his seat in an angry voice. "He's my sister's son just like you are. I am not about to have this conversation ever again. He is one of us."

When Tommy returns, Sonny is sitting back down. Joey, standing, nodding his head while scratching his forehead, "Bring that thing over here!" Sonny demands.

"This is my black operation computer," Tommy says.

"What does that mean?" Sonny asks.

Tommy smirks, "The less you know the better off you are."

Sonny laughs. "You sound like one of us."

"I am a Grasso. What's the account number that got hacked?" Tommy asks while powering up his computer. Sonny looks over at Joey as he reads off the account numbers.

*   *   *

Back in Chicago, Octavius is rewriting the program to destroy all information that could possibly lead back to them. Brown is standing over him. "Is it done?"

"Nope." He continues to type very rapidly. He turns and looks at Brown and taps the enter button. "It's done now."

Tommy looks at Sonny and taps the enter key. "It's done. It could take some time. However, I do think we'll find it."

Sonny leans back in his seat. "We're going to need a new security person to protect the accounts. I'll talk to the other bosses, if you pull this off." Joey sits across the room furious that he couldn't get it done.

* * *

Three months later in the dead of winter Octavius is sitting in a five-star restaurant with Sharon from the dealership. Sharon is looking like a fashion model. She is slightly older than Octavius by a few years, no matter heads just kept turning every time she enters a room. Her slim, curvy frame fit that Vera Wang dress like body paint. Octavius rocking all Gucci from the watch, clothes and shoes has started to look the part of a young millionaire.

Stanley Fisher sits across the room trying to build up his courage to go talk with Octavius. He knew some funny business had taken place as he sat there thinking, *How could this little piece of shit go from rags to riches? He has no more than a bachelor's degree in computer engineering. Maybe he signed on with one of the major companies ... NO!*

The market is full of tech people. Not as good as Octavius though. He jumps up and makes his way over to the table. He extends his hand to Octavius. Octavius grabs his napkin and wipes his mouth before extending his hand.

Octavius smiles. "How's it going, Stanley Fisher? Let me introduce you to Sharon."

Stanley shakes Sharon's hand gently. "Nice to meet you, Sharon."

"Nice to meet you as well," Sharon responds.

Octavius sips his water. "So, Fish, what brings you to my table?"

Stanley Fisher, in the most humbling voice, "I was wondering if you would reconsider my Dad's offer with a signing bonus?"

Octavius leans back in his chair and closes his eyes for a moment. "Okay, I just thought about it."

Fisher, with a glimmer of hope in his eyes, "Okay … meaning that you'll do it?"

Octavius quickly shuts down the thought of going back to work. "Okay as in I thought about it and NO!"

Sharon giggles slightly. "Octavius, do you have to be so insensitive?"

Mr. Fisher, humiliated, turns quickly walking back to his table. He could hear them speaking as he walked back to his table. "I'm never going to work for them again. He knows nothing about the work he does," Octavius says.

Sharon spoke through her laughter, "You are just so wrong for saying that."

"Not really, if you know all the hell he put me through."

*   *   *

Back on the East Coast Tommy walks into Sonny's office with excitement in his voice, carrying his computer, "Uncle Sonny, I got it."

Sonny sits up with a disturbed look on his face. "What do you have, Tommy?"

"I have the signature of the person who stole the money." Tommy quickly opens his laptop computer. Working quickly, he pulls up a couple of sites.

Sonny, unfazed about what Tommy is saying because he has just gotten a phone call from one of the family bosses, has informed Sonny that the families have heard about the money. Sonny snaps out of his daze. "What are you saying?"

Tommy, pointing at the screen, says, "I'm saying whoever took the money is connected to Computer World and this website Iamhot.com. For some reason this person forgot to remove his signature from these sites in Chicago."

Sonny leans back in his chair exhaling deeply. He pats Tommy on the back, "Great job, nephew." Sonny rubs his palms together in deep thought. "I haven't talked to Barone in years. I guess that I need to give him a call to let him know we're coming to Chi-Town."

"Who is Barone?" Tommy asks.

"Bone Barone is one of the most infamous guys I've ever met. He also happens to be the head of the families in Chicago. Tell Joey to get a few of the guys together. We're going to Chicago."

Tommy exits the room. Sonny picks up his cell phone reluctantly and calls out to Barone. The phone rings one time before Barone answers in a raspy voice, "Hello!"

"Hey, Barone! This is Sonny!"

"Hey, Sonny! How the hell are you? I haven't heard from any of the East Coast families in years."

"Barone, I have a problem in Chicago that I need to come fix. I was hoping that you would sanction a visit."

"Sonny, we go back twenty years. Of course I'll do that for you. How soon are you coming, and how many?"

"This Friday."

"Sonny, you have my blessing and the key to the city. It's not often when a 20-year-old friend reaches out to another."

"Thanks, Barone! See you on Friday."

The next day it's cold out and Brown and Octavius meet at the local coffee shop. Octavius enters the place like he's the owner. Brown already seated is waiting on Octavius to walk over to his table. Brown chuckles when he notices the change in Octavius' walk.

"What's good, Bro?" Octavius looks around the room. "What are you laughing about?"

Brown smirks. "Nothing. Have a seat. I have someone looking to move the money for us in ten days. We just have to act normal and not go crazy spending money that we don't have. You understand?"

"Bro, you talking to me like I'm slow or something. I hear you loud and clear."

Brown sips on his coffee. "So what do you plan on doing once you get your money?"

"Hell, I'm going to ball till I fall, you feel me?"

"No, I don't feel you. On a more serious note, have you given it any thought?" A young, beautiful woman walks pass catching Octavius' attention. He follows her with his eyes all the way to the counter. She smiles looking in Octavius' direction. Octavius waves, and she frowns as the guy she's smiling at approaches her at the counter. Brown starts laughing. "Dude, pick your face up! Everything that looks good ain't good for you!"

"Ha Ha! She was feeling me though," Octavius says.

"If you say so. You have a few days to decide what you need to do. I need to make some arrangements with Ivan's family to get him some cash."

"How's his case coming along?"

"Not good! He gets sentenced next week."

"DAMN! Bro, I don't know if I could do time," Octavius says. Brown gives Octavius a real strange look after his statement. Octavius seeing the look on Brown's face, "I mean if I have to, a brother gotta do what he gotta do. You feel me?"

Brown nods in agreement, but his thoughts are completely different. "Yeah, I understand where you're coming from."

Octavius takes a bite off his croissant thinking to himself, *Damn I shouldn't have said that.* "So what's up with the girl you met in Virginia?"

"She's good," Brown says.

"That's it? Give me some details! When do I get to meet her? You know Khloe is waiting in the wing for some type of action," Octavius states.

"Damn this some good coffee," Brown says.

"It's like that?" Octavius asks.

"You'll meet her when it's time."

"Straight like that, huh?"

"In your words, that's it that's all."

"You're something else, B. Real talk though I want to thank you for showing me another side of life. You have been like a big brother and mentor to me. Thanks, Big Bro." Octavius closes his hand and pounds on his chest, "It's all love over here."

Brown isn't really used to that type of friendship. "Why you getting all sentimental did somebody die or something?" Brown starts laughing.

Octavius unamused just gives him a hard stare. He quickly scans the room before whispering. "Brown, what you know about credit profile numbers?"

"Not much ... why?"

"Cassie and Khloe have been getting some information on how to get it done."

"You really need to stay away from that. The process involves too much paperwork, and that poses a greater risk for getting caught. Besides cash is king!"

"Why you say that cash is king? In today's society you can't do anything with cash. You can't make a reservation, shop online, rent a car, and at some places you can't even buy gas."

"The reason I say cash is king is because you don't need a signature. Therefore, you can pretty much move around without being noticed. Besides that, you have cash now, why worry about it?"

Octavius finishes up his sandwich in deep thought about what Brown has just said. His cell phone vibrates with a text from Cassie. *HEY THERE! CAN YOU COME BY THE CONDO THIS EVENING? WE NEED TO TALK, AND I BOUGHT SOME WHIPPED CREAM FOR YOU!*

Octavius smirks as he responds. *THAT'S FUNNY! I'LL STOP BY AROUND 8 THIS EVENING.*

She quickly responds. *SMOOCHES!*

Octavius jumps up from the table. "I'm out, Bro. Get up with me later."

"I sure will," Brown says.

Octavius turns to walk out of the coffee shop, but Brown couldn't get that comment out his head. *"I can't do time."* Brown shakes it off and gets up, leaving the coffee shop.

* * *

Downtown, later that afternoon at the Water Tower, Cassie and Khloe are shopping. They turn heads as they stroll through the Water Tower carrying designer purses and wearing Tiffany's jewelry. Khloe's looking at one of the store mannequin's outfit, and Cassie is texting when someone bumps Cassie sending her cell phone crashing to the floor. "Bitch!" Cassie yells, as she reaches for her cell phone.

Khloe quickly turns around to see what's going on. When Cassie starts to rise from the floor, she notices three women standing right in front of her. Khloe stares at the girls before asking Cassie, "Is your phone broken? If so we can get another while we're downtown?"

Cassie quickly recalls who the girls are. "So you must didn't get enough that night at Nympho's! So what's up?" Cassie quickly puts her bags down making a scene. People start gathering with cell phones to record, anticipating a fight is brewing.

China is more aggressive feeling like they got the best of her because she was high off pills. Tasha, more of the spokesperson for the group, "No, it's not like that at all Sweet Thang."

Holly, a true friend and follower of Tasha, just stands there waiting for it to jump off. A young man standing in the crowd holding his cell phone yells, "LET'S GET IT CRACK'IN! WORLD STAR!!"

Instantly, Cassie realizes what's about to happen will only bring negative attention to her and Khloe. "No! We're not about to put on a show for these people."

Khloe picks up her bags from the floor. "You are so right, gorgeous. Let's move around. The air is kind of ugly around here." She was looking towards Holly.

Holly giggles looking at Khloe. "Get you some ass before you speak about somebody being unattractive. There's nothing less attractive than a flat ass."

The crowd is dispersing as mall security is approaching. The same guy who yelled out World Star walks pass Khloe. "She's wrong! Your ass isn't flat, but it is small."

Khloe offended. "Move back, CREEP!"

After everyone walks away, Holly walks up to Khloe and Cassie. Cassie speaks with an attitude, "WHAT?"

"Look! It's obvious that we are all nice looking women. I was just hoping that we could get along. Take my number. It's too many men out here to fight over one."

Cassie slightly irritated, "He's my man. That's it and that's all that needs to be said. But, I'm going to take your number just maybe there's something we can do together." Holly gives Cassie her number as she programs it into her cell phone.

"Okay, Boo, take care!" Holly turns to catch up with China and Tasha.

Khloe stands looking confused. "Okay! What the fuck just happened? Really? You took that Bitch's number? Where they do that at? Right after we were about to whoop them bitches."

Cassie looks at Khloe, "You know sometimes you can do a little too much."

"REALLY, CASSIE?" They pick up their bags and head for the exit.

"Khloe, them girls have their stuff together. I was sizing them up, looking at their gear. Those bitches had on designer everything from the shoes down to the purses. That bitch, China, had on some Christian Louboutin boots. They're getting paid out here, and we are barely scratching the surface."

"You are tripping! You know strippers make a lot of cash. I'm not about to strip for no cash."

"You already do. What do you call what you're doing with old man, Tyrone?"

"That's different. He's my Sugar Daddy."

"Yeah, but he's old enough to be your father's daddy."

Khloe laughs. "Girl, you stupid. He's not that old."

Cassie laughs. "Pretty damn close." They walk out of the Water Tower quickly, zipping their coats on this cold early evening.

*   *   *

That Friday afternoon Bone Barone sends one of his drivers to pick up Sonny and the guys from the airport. Sonny and the guys walk out of the airport. Barone's driver, Tony, jumps out of the Cadillac truck to greet them. Sonny shakes Tony's hand then embraces him with a big hug. "It's been years since I've been in Chicago." He takes a look around. "It sure has changed. This airport is beautiful. One thing that hasn't changed is the weather. Hell, it's cold out here."

Tony smiles while opening the truck door for Sonny to get in. Sonny jumps in, rubbing his hands together to generate some heat. "Okay, first things first. We need to get over to the rental car company."

"Barone said that you don't have to rent a car. I can drive you around to where you need to go."

"No disrespect to Barone or his family, but this is not a social visit," Sonny exclaimed.

"No matter the reason I'm here to do whatever needs to be done," Tony says.

Joey jumps in the front seat. "It's really cold here today. The luggage is in the back of the truck. Hey, Tony, with all this homeland security crap, we weren't able to pack the way we normally would. You think...." Tony just nods his head in agreement, as he looks how much the city has changed. "Tony, do you have a piece on you now?"

"Yes, Sir! It's our family custom to keep it at all times."

"Good. Let's swing over by this place. What's the place again, Tommy?"

"Computer World located downtown. I can GPS it for you," Tommy answers, removing his laptop from his backpack.

"No, I'm good. We'll be there in no time," Tony responds.

It's just about closing time, and Mr. Fisher is looking out the window at the snow flurries when a Black SUV pulls up in front of the store. Mr. Fisher has let the other employees leave early because of the snow storm warning. Five guys enter the store wearing suits and one wearing blue jeans and a jacket carrying a backpack. Mr. Fisher feeling good. It's closing time, ready to go home. "Hey, Fellas, its closing time, but I'll be more than happy to assist you. How can I help you?"

No one cracked a smile or mumbled a word. At that moment Fisher sensed that something was wrong. "Okay ... who are you and why are you here?"

Tommy steps forward, opening his laptop, "Is this your signature bird?"

Fisher leans down to take a closer look at the screen always wanting to take credit for Octavius work. "Why yes that's our signature bird."

Sonny nods his head, and quickly, the guys go to work. One locks the door, the other flips the closed sign, and Joe Jr. shows Fisher the pistol. Sonny, very angry, steps closer to the counter. "Where's my money?"

Fisher has no clue what is going on tries to explain, "What money?"

Danny Boy walks behind Fisher knocking him out cold. When Fisher awakes, he's tied up in the back office chair. Tommy has hacked some of Fisher's old accounts to reveal to Sonny this is the guy. Sonny walks up to Fisher. "This will be the last time I ask you nicely. Where is my money?"

Fisher pleads, "I don't know what money you're talking about."

Tommy interjects, "The money your little signature bird ran off with."

"Oh I see now. That's not my bird. It's one of my former employee's birds. His name is Octavius Smith. He would be the only person I know who could do something like this. He's great at computers, but he isn't that type of guy. Oh wait a minute. Lately, he has been real flamboyant, driving a new BMW, taking all the ladies out to five-star restaurants. Yeah!! It has to be him."

Sonny is convinced. He is telling the truth because they hadn't even roughed him up. Sonny laughs. "Do you know who we are?"

Fisher afraid but also wanting to get back Octavius for his disrespect, "No, Sir, and I don't need to know. The less I know the less I can say."

"Say about what?" Sonny asks.

"Anything," Fisher states.

"Sonny, I see where an employee here was Octavius Smith in his files, but there's no address," Tommy says.

"West Loop new development over by the United Center more so off Ashland and Monroe. That's all I know. Oh yeah, and one more thing, his girlfriend, Cassie Rose, runs a website Iamhot.com. Now that's it!" Fisher exclaims.

Sonny shakes his head, "What happened to all the tough guys in the world. Danny Boy, take care of this situation."

Danny Boy walks over to Fisher and chokes him from behind. Fisher flailing, trying to get away. However, Danny Boy puts him to sleep. They all turn to walk out of Computer World. The guys all go by Barone's sports bar. Sonny immediately greets Barone with a kiss on the cheek.

"It's been years since we have seen one another," Barone says with a huge smile on his face.

Sonny's eyes light up for a second, "Bone, I gotta tell you this has been one hell of a year with my sister passing away. Now some Schmuck thinks he can take millions from the family and get away with it. These fucking millennial babies think they can just do whatever the fuck they want without consequences. I'll tell you I'm getting too old for this shit."

Barone, with a look of concern, "Sonny, come sit and have a drink for old times' sake." They walk over to the bar and share some memories while Tommy tries to track down Cassie.

After about thirty minutes of laughing and drinking, Tommy approaches Sonny. Sonny has a tender moment looking at Tommy. "Barone, this is my sister's boy, Tommy. Tommy, this is Mr. Barone."

"Damn, Sonny! He looks just like her. Tommy, your mom is a very sweet woman, and from the looks of it, she raised you right!" Barone states.

Tommy, slightly irritated by the moment, "Sonny, I found the girl."

Sonny snaps, "Hey, don't be disrespectful to my friend. He paid you a compliment. You at least owe him a response."

"Sorry, Mr. Barone, but Sonny told me this was a life or death situation so I'm only focused on the business," Tommy says sincerely.

Barone pats Tommy on the back, "I understand. Now Sonny, what's this about life or death?" Sonny goes on to explain what happened, and Barone recalls the incident on the news.

"Okay, Sonny, okay. Tony, you get a couple of the guys and go with Joey and his crew. I want this bitch found tonight. They must not realize who they're fucking with. Bring the bitch and anyone she is with back to the meat packing plant. Capiche?!"

"Yes, Bone, I understand!" Tony replies. Sonny rubs his forehead.

"Don't worry, Sonny, we're going get that money back!" Barone says.

"Hey, Danny Boy! Go back over to Computer World and grab that guy too."

Joey, with a strange look, "For what, Sonny? He's dead!"

"No, Joey! Sonny just said put him to sleep."

That's what I did!" Danny Boy replies.

"Christ! He wanted you to kill him!" Joey says.

"Not true. If so, I wouldn't be telling you to pick him up. Besides he knows who we're looking for," Sonny responds.

They head for the door like soldiers on one another's heels. They pull up in front of Computer World. Danny Boy runs inside to find Fisher still tied up in the chair. Fisher sees Danny Boy and tries to play dead, but Danny Boy has already seen him move. He pulls his pistol out and unties Fisher taking him out to the van. Fisher, scared for his life, "Fellas, I told you everything I know. Please don't kill me!"

No one replies to Fisher's crying. They pull up in front of Cassie's building. Danny Boy points the pistol at Fisher. "Now you're going to help us get to her."

"Okay! Not a problem!" Fisher responds.

They sit and watch the building from both sides of the street, some in the SUV and the others in the van. They watch car after car for over an hour. Cassie still hasn't shown up, and it's getting late.

"Are you sure this is the right place?" Joey asks Tommy.

"According to the website and account they have in the system, this is it!" Tommy states.

Moments later an Uber driver pulls up letting out two young ladies. Fisher, frantically, "That's her!"

They quickly slide the van door open. "Fisher, you're going to have her to walk back over towards the van, and we'll take it from there. Know that your life depends on this."

Fisher quickly walks up with Danny Boy on his heels. They approach the Uber driver taking packages out of the truck. Cassie is caught off guard when she turns and Fisher is standing there in the cold without a jacket. Khloe gives Fisher and Danny Boy a strange look. "Cassie, who is this guy?"

"Octavius' old boss. He's harmless."

Fisher whispers to Cassie, "Hey, I need to talk to you for a second?"

"What, Fisher? Octavius told me about the job offer. He doesn't want it!" Cassie says bitterly.

"It's not about that. He's in a little bit of trouble!" Fisher says.

Cassie panics. "OH MY GOD! Is he okay?"

Khloe rushing Cassie, "Girl, come on. I have to use the bathroom. NOW!"

Cassie gives Khloe the keys, "Go on up there, Girl. I'll be right up."

Cassie walks off with Fisher, and Khloe rushes into the building to get out of the cold. "Now, Fisher, what's going on with Octavius?" Cassie asks.

"He's in a lot of trouble."

The van door slides open, and Danny Boy pushes Cassie inside leaving Fisher out on the sidewalk. She screams as the van speeds off. Fisher keeps walking like nothing happened. The guys speed to the meat packing plant. Once inside Sonny and Barone are sitting there waiting.

"So this is Ms. Iamhot.com? Fucking kids are stupid. They put all their business out there for the world to see then wonder how someone could know who they are." Sonny just shakes his head.

Barone walks over to Cassie trying to intimidate her. "There are two ways to get things done around here ... the hard way or the easy way. The choice is yours. Now where is that boyfriend of yours?"

Cassie doesn't say a word. Barone smirks looking at Cassie, "Okay, have it your way. Now you are about to see how I got the name Bone Barone. Tony get the duct tape and start the machine."

Cassie thinks she is about to be raped and closes her eyes as the machine starts. The machine is louder than a semi- truck. Barone walks closer to the meat grinder grabbing the white smock and goggles. "Bring her over here." Barone demands.

Joey and Tony take her over to the machine. Cassie kicking and screaming, "PLEASE NO!! PLEASE NO!! SOMEBODY HELP ME!! PLEASE, LORD, NO!!!" Tears stream down Cassie's face. Barone grabs a leg of lamb tossing it into the grinder, blood shoots everywhere on Cassie. Barone gives a signal to cut the machine off. Cassie's in tears, "I'll do whatever you ask me! Please no more!"

Barone removes his goggles and smock with a smirk, "That's why they call me Bone Barone. I don't have a problem throwing things in the machine. That means you, pretty little lady."

Some of the guys laugh, and the others couldn't stomach the blood so they had to step out. Sonny walks over to Cassie, "Call him on your cell phone right now."

Cassie, trying to regain her composure, dials Octavius' number very slowly, as Barone instructs her on where to meet. The phone rings! "Hey, Babe! What's up?"

"Hey, Sweetie! I know it's late, but I need you to meet me at the sports bar on Ashland and Lake. Can you do that for me please?" Cassie asks.

Octavius could tell something was wrong, but couldn't figure it out. "Are you okay?"

"Yeah! Khloe and I had a big fight," Cassie says.

"REALLY? Okay, Babe! I'm on the way. I'll be there in about thirty minutes." Octavius hangs up the phone and hightails it over to the sports bar. When he arrives, the bar is packed with guys watching Ultimate Fighting Main Event. Octavius glances around the room at all the huge monitors in this midsize bar. He walks over to the bar, takes a seat, and pulls out his cell phone to call Cassie. Two men in suits walk up behind Octavius. Octavius quickly turns to see the two men. Joey shows him a picture of Cassie tied up. "If you want to see her alive again, you need to get up and follow us!"

Octavius afraid tries to cause a scene to draw some attention. "Who the fuck are you?"

Tony leans forward whispering in Octavius' ear, "The one who's going to kill your girl, if you don't get up now." Tony grabs the back of Octavius' arm leading him to the back of the restaurant. Once in the back room Tommy is there with two computer monitors setup. Cassie is lying on the table of a meat grinder. Octavius is forcefully sat down at the monitor next to Tommy. Tommy calmly turns to Octavius, "You do know why you are here, right?"

"I have no clue what's going on here, but you're making a huge mistake!" Octavius states.

Joey walks over to Octavius and smacks him in the mouth, "Now do you know?"

Octavius' mouth starts bleeding, Tommy hands him a paper towel. "The next thing that starts bleeding around here won't be able to be stopped with a paper towel. My advice to you is to return the money that you have stolen!" Tommy says.

Octavius wipes the blood from his mouth looking at Cassie on the monitor thinking to himself, *"She didn't have anything to do with this."* He begins typing away into the accounts that the money was wired too. He has no luck with the accounts. For some odd reason the accounts are at minimum balance of $1500. He quickly pulls up the withdrawals on the accounts and sees that the money was withdrawn yesterday. He falls back in his seat. *"Fucking Brown got me, and I'm a dead man!"*

Tommy quickly taps into the accounts to see the funds have been withdrawn. He calls Sonny on the cell. "Sonny, someone else is involved. I cross-checked the account, and the money was there as of yesterday."

Sonny is furious! "Tell him to watch the monitor. Danny Boy shoot her in the leg."

Danny Boy walks over to Cassie on the table, pulls out his pistol, and aims it at her leg. Octavius tries to turn his head the second Danny Boy shoots Cassie in the leg. He watches Cassie scream from under the duct tape. Tears start to form in her eyes as she cries for mercy.

Barone, anxious to get involved, "Start the machine."

Octavius couldn't take anymore yells out, "Enough ... I'll call him! He double-crossed me anyway." Octavius removes his cell phone from his pocket to call Brown.

Brown answers. "Hey, Dude! I've been waiting to hear from you. I didn't think it would be this soon."

Octavius is fighting back his tears, but his voice is shaky, "Bro, they're going to kill me and Cassie, if we don't give back the money. Why did you take the money, Bro? I need it! They're going to kill us.

Cassie's already been shot in the leg. Where are you, and where's the money, Bro? Please!"

"Just think back to last week when we were talking and you said, *"I can't do any time. It's whatever! I can't go to jail."* Yeah, I decided at that moment you couldn't be trusted, so I took the money!" Brown replies calmly.

"You're talking to a dead man, if the money isn't returned in the next hour. Give me the account numbers! Please, Brown!"

Joey snatches the phone away from Octavius speaking in a very threatening way, "Look here ... this kid's blood is on your hands, if he dies. Stop fucking around, and give up the account numbers."

"Okay! Kill him and his bitch! This way I can keep all the money!" Brown hangs up the phone. He instantly opens up his computer to track Octavius' GPS that he installed without Octavius' knowing. The phone pings to Octavius' whereabouts. He quickly triggers the silent alarm at the bar sending the local authorities straight to the bar. The fire department and police get there at the same time rushing inside. Octavius hears the sirens. Joey, Tommy, and Tony try to rush out the back door with Octavius. The place is surrounded.

The Feds have been watching Barone and his organization from across the street. They quickly intervene taking over the situation finding an arsenal of weapons. The Feds take Octavius to the back room for an interrogation. Octavius tells them about Cassie over at the meat plant. They quickly dispatch a team to raid the plant. They convince Octavius to cooperate. He takes the team back to Brown's condo. The Feds stop at the front desk to see if James Brown is listed as an occupant. Oddly enough, he is not.

"No, we don't have anyone listed by that name in our units," Security says.

They rush up to the 11th floor and pause before ramming the door down with the battering ram. "This is the police!" Once in the apartment they discover it is vacant. Octavius stands there in disbelief. "What the fuck?"

The lead officer asks, "Mr. Smith, where's the other apartment you were telling us about?"

"It's around the corner, Apartment number 1111." Octavius says, leading the way.

"Ram it down!" The lead officer demands.

Once inside the condo is found vacant, not one piece of furniture. "When did he do this? I was just here a couple days ago." Octavius asks shaking his head.

The lead officer gets a call on his radio, "10-4. Your girlfriend is going to be okay. She lost a lot of blood, but she'll make a full recovery."

"Thank, God!" Octavius says.

"Not yet. You have the right to remain silent. You have the right to counsel. If you cannot afford one, one will be appointed by the U.S. Court."

Octavius is transported to MCC Chicago, where he meets a guy named Ivan. Ivan is the guy who used to sell Brown the credit card numbers. The Feds can't charge Sonny Grasso with any crime or Bone Barone. They are free on bond until their court date. However, the Feds keep on pushing Octavius for information and force him to cop-out for 36 months for credit card fraud.

The Feds have no idea what Brown looks like. He is very smart, never taking pictures and staying away from social media.

Cassie is at home with Khloe recovering from one of her three surgeries when her cell phone rings anonymous. "Khloe, pass me that phone please! I don't see a number. It's probably just a bill collector. Hello!"

"Hey, Sunshine!"

"Who is this?" Cassie asks.

"Wow! It hasn't been that long."

"I don't have time to play games. I'm in a lot of pain. Who is this before I hang up?" Cassie states.

"Hang up, Girl! We're too old to play fucking games!" Khloe says.

"Same old Khloe, huh?"

"BROWN! Is this you?" Cassie asks.

"Yes, Cassie. How's my dude doing?"

"He's holding up okay. He just got sentenced to 36 months for credit card fraud. I went to see him last week. He said that he's locked up with someone else that knows you named Ivan." Cassie replies. The call drops. "Hello? Hello? Dammit ... the call dropped ... or did he just hang up on me?" Cassie questions.

"Maybe he'll call back, then maybe he won't. Hell … I guess everybody doesn't get caught and go to jail. I wouldn't call back if I got away with millions of dollars!" Khloe responds.

Cassie, sitting on the couch, gives Khloe a strange look while lightly massaging her injury. "Oh well, if he doesn't call back, we'll just have to get it Crack'in II."

THE END

Order at <u>www.mcclurepublishing.com</u> and other leading book stores.

Kevin Whitaker is also the author of his debut novel "The Party Girl" and his second novel "SCORN – The Legacy."